Carol Marinelli recently filled in a form asking for her job title. Thrilled to be able to put down her answer, she put 'writer'. Then it asked what Carol did for relaxation and she put down the truth—'writing'. The third question asked for her hobbies. Well, not wanting to look obsessed, she crossed her fingers and answered 'swimming'—but, given that the chlorine in the pool does terrible things to her highlights, I'm sure you can guess the real answer!

Books by Carol Marinelli

Mills & Boon Modern Romance

Billionaires & One-Night Heirs

The Innocent's Secret Baby
Bound by the Sultan's Baby

One Night With Consequences

The Sheikh's Baby Scandal

The Billionaire's Legacy

Di Sione's Innocent Conquest

Irresistible Russian Tycoons

The Price of His Redemption
The Cost of the Forbidden
Billionaire Without a Past
Return of the Untamed Billionaire

Mills & Boon Medical Romance

Their Secret Royal Baby

Paddington Children's Hospital

Their One Night Baby

The London Primary Hospital

Playboy on Her Christmas List

Visit the Author Profile page
at millsandboon.co.uk for more titles.

For my wonderful editor Flo Nicoll.
Thank you for being you.
Carol xxx

There was a gap between their chests, but so in tune was Sophie with Bastiano's every move that she felt as if their bodies touched.

It was time to stay or go. Sophie knew that. Even at this stage she could smooth it over and make her farewells.

Or she could meet those lips and discover bliss.

'Come here,' Bastiano moaned, and his hand came up and pulled her head down to his.

Always she had avoided such contact, and yet now she craved it.

His mouth was soft, and the dark shadow of his skin did not make her skin crawl with its tickle; instead it was rough and delicious and matched the building desire in her.

Now, instead of resisting, she opened her lips, wanting and willing.

His tongue felt like a reward as it coiled around hers. They tasted each other, and they inflamed each other—and not just with their mouths. He was stroking her breast through the fabric of her dress and Sophie ached for bed.

His bed.

Billionaires & One-Night Heirs

Secret babies they are determined to claim!

Raul, Alim and Bastiano—
three billionaires renowned the world over
for their charisma and commanding ways.

Lydia, Gabi and Sophie—three innocents
who cannot resist their seductive appeal.

And when sizzling nights lead to nine-month
consequences there is no other option—
these billionaires *will* claim their heirs!

The Innocent's Secret Baby

Bound by the Sultan's Baby

Sicilian's Baby of Shame

Available now!

You won't want to miss this addictive new trilogy
from Carol Marinelli!

SICILIAN'S
BABY OF SHAME

BY
CAROL MARINELLI

This is a work of fiction. Names, characters, places, locations and
incidents are purely fictional and bear no relationship to any real
life individuals, living or dead, or to any actual places, business
establishments, locations, events or incidents. Any resemblance is
entirely coincidental.

First Published in Great Britain 2017
By Mills & Boon, an imprint of HarperCollins*Publishers*
1 London Bridge Street, London, SE1 9GF

© 2017 Carol Marinelli

ISBN: 978-0-263-06925-9

Our policy is to use papers that are natural, renewable and recyclable
products and made from wood grown in sustainable forests. The logging
and manufacturing processes conform to the legal environmental
regulations of the country of origin.

Printed and bound in Great Britain
by CPI Antony Rowe, Chippenham, Wiltshire

PROLOGUE

BASTIANO CONTI HAD been born hungry.

And born a problem.

His mother had died giving birth to him and had never disclosed who his father was. All she had owned had been left to him—a ring.

It was Italian gold with a small emerald in its centre and some seed pearls dotted around it.

Bastiano's uncle, who had four children of his own, had first suggested that the nuns raise the orphaned baby who'd lain crying in the small maternity ward in the Valley of Casta. There was a convent that overlooked the Sicilian Strait and orphans had usually been sent there.

But the convent was on its last legs.

The nurses were busy but occasionally one would take pity and hold Bastiano a little longer than it took to feed him.

Occasionally.

'Familia,' the priest had said to his uncle. 'Everyone knows that the Contis look after their own.'

The Contis ruled the valley to the west and the Di Savos held the east.

Loyalty to their own was paramount, the priest told him. And so, after a stern talk from the priest, Bastiano's *zio* and his reluctant wife had taken the little bastard to their house but it had never, for Bastiano, been a home.

Always Bastiano had been considered an outsider. If something had gone wrong, then he'd been the first to be blamed and the last to be forgiven.

If there had been four brioches for lunch, they had not been split to make five.

Bastiano had done without.

Sitting in school next to Raul Di Savo, Bastiano had started to understand why.

'What would your parents save in a fire?' Sister Francesca had asked her class. 'Raul?'

Raul had shrugged.

'Your father,' she prompted, 'what would be the first thing that Gino reached for?'

'His wine.'

The class had laughed and Sister Francesca, growing more exasperated with each passing moment, had turned her attention from Raul.

'Bastiano,' she snapped. 'Who would your *zia* save?'

His serious grey eyes had lifted to hers and Bastiano had frowned even as he'd given his response. 'Her children.'

'Correct.'

She had turned back to the board and Bastiano had sat there, still frowning, for indeed it was the correct answer—his *zia* would save her children. But not him.

He would never be first.

However, aged seven, Bastiano was sent to collect the brioches and the baker's wife ruffled his hair and so unused to affection was he that his face lit up and she said that he had a cute smile.

'You do too,' Bastiano told her, and she laughed.

'Here.' She gave him a sweet cannoli just for brightening her morning and Bastiano and Raul sat on the hill and ate the gooey treat.

The boys should have been sworn enemies—for generations the Contis and the Di Savos had fought over the vines and properties in the valley—yet Bastiano and Raul became firm friends.

The small encounter at the baker's was enough for Bastiano to learn that he could get by better on charm.

Oh, a smile worked wonders, and later he learnt to flirt with his eyes and was rewarded with something far sweeter than cannoli.

Despite their families' protests, Bastiano and Raul remained friends. They would often sit high on the hill near the now vacant convent and drink cheap wine. As they looked out over the valley, Raul told him of the beatings his mother endured and admitted that he was reluctant to leave for university in Rome.

'Stay, then.'

It was that simple to Bastiano. If he'd had a mother, or someone who cared for him, he would not leave.

And he did not want Raul to go, though of course Bastiano did not admit that.

Raul left.

One morning, walking down the street, he saw Gino storm out of Raul's house, shouting and leaving the front door open.

Raul was gone and, given what his friend had told him, Bastiano thought he ought to check that his mother was okay.

'Signora Di Savo…' He knocked on the open door but she did not answer.

He could hear that she was crying.

His *zia* and *zio* called her unhinged but Maria Di Savo had always been kind to Bastiano.

Concerned, he walked inside and she was kneeling on the floor of the kitchen, crying.

'Hey.' He poured her a drink and then he got a cloth and ran it under the water and pressed it to the bruise on her eye.

'Do you want me to call someone?' he offered.

'No.'

He helped her to stand and she leant on him and cried and Bastiano did not know what to do.

'Why don't you leave him?' he asked.

'I've tried many times.'

Bastiano frowned because Raul had always said that he'd pleaded with her to leave yet she'd always refused.

'Could you go and stay with Raul in Rome?' Bastiano suggested.

'He doesn't want me there. He left me,' Maria sobbed. 'No one wants me.'

'That's not true.'

'You mean it?'

She looked up then and he went to correct her to say that what he had meant was that he was sure there were people who wanted her...

Not him.

She put a hand up to his face and held his cheek. 'You're so handsome.'

Maria ran a hand through his thick black hair and it did *not* feel like when the baker's wife had; this felt more than an affectionate ruffle and, confused, Bastiano removed her hand and stepped back. 'I have to go,' he told her.

'Not yet.'

She wore just a slip and her breast was a little exposed; he did not want Maria to be embarrassed when she realised that she was on display, so he turned to leave.

'Please don't go,' she called out to him.

'I have to go to work.'

He had left school and worked now in the bar that was a front for the seedier dealings of his *zio*.

'Please, Bastiano...' Maria begged. She reached for his arm and when he stopped she came around so that she stood in front of him. 'Oh,' she apologised as she looked down and saw that her breast was exposed to him, but Bastiano did not look. He was still pretending that he had not noticed.

And she would cover herself now, Bastiano thought, yet she did not. In fact, she took his hand and placed it on her plump, ripe skin.

He was good with the girls but in those cases he was the seducer. Maria was around forty, he guessed, and, for heaven's sake, she was the mother of his best friend.

'Signora Di Savo...' Her hand pressed his as he went to remove it.

'Maria,' she said, and her voice was low and husky. He could feel and hear her deep breathing and when she removed her hand, Bastiano's remained on her breast.

'You're hard,' Maria said, feeling him.

'Gino might—'

'He won't be back till dinner.'

Bastiano was usually the leader and instigator, but not on this hot morning. Maria was back on her knees but this time by her own doing. It was over within minutes.

As he left, he swore he would never return there.

But that very afternoon Bastiano made a trip to the pharmacy for protection, and an hour later they were in bed.

Hot, forbidden, intense—they met whenever they could, though it was never enough for Maria.

'We're getting out,' Bastiano told her. He had been paid and, if all else failed, he had his mother's ring. He could not stand the thought of her with Gino for even a moment longer.

'We can't,' she told him, even as she asked to see the ring and he watched as she slipped it on.

'If you love me,' Maria said, 'you would want me to have nice things.'

'Maria, give me back the ring.'

It was all he had of his mother but still Maria did not relent. Bastiano left.

He walked up the hill to the convent and sat looking out, trying to figure it all out. All his life he had wanted a taste of this elusive thing called love, only to find out he did not care for it. It was Bastiano who now wanted out.

And he wanted his mother's ring.

He stood, walking with purpose to the town below, where he saw it unfold.

A car driving at speed took a bend too fast. '*Stolto*,' he muttered, and called the driver a fool as he watched him take another bend…and then the car careered from the road.

Bastiano ran in the direction of the smoking wreck but as he approached he was held back and told that it was Gino's car that had been in the accident.

'Gino?' Bastiano checked.

'No!' a woman who worked in the bar shouted. 'I called Maria to say that Gino was on his way home and angry. He had found out about you! She took the car and—'

Maria's death and the aftermath had not painted Bastiano in a very flattering light.

Raul returned from Rome and on the eve of the funeral they stood on the hill where once they had sat as boys.

'You had your pick of the valley!' Raul could barely contain his fury.

'I went to check on her—'

But Raul did not want to hear that his mother had been the seducer. 'And you turned on that fake charm…' Raul had seen him in action after all. He knew how Bastiano could summon even the shyest woman with his eyes and melt restraint with a smile. 'I was a fool to trust you,' Raul said. 'You as good as killed her.'

Yes, he was the first to be blamed and the last to be forgiven.

'Stay away from the funeral,' Raul warned him.

But Bastiano could not.

And the next day things went from bad to worse. After a bloody fight at the graveside, it later transpired that half of Maria's money had been left to Bastiano.

Raul, once his friend, now accused Bastiano of en-gineering Maria's death and swore the rest of his days would be devoted to bringing him down.

'You're nothing, Conti,' Raul told him. 'You never have been and, even with my mother's money, you never will be.'

'Watch me,' Bastiano warned.

It is said that it takes a village to raise a child.

The Valley of Casta had never really been kind to Bas-tiano, but when the entire population considered you a cheat, a liar, a seducer, a bastard…that's what you become.

So, when a drunken Gino came to confront him, in-stead of taking it on the chin, Bastiano fought back, and when Gino called Maria a whore, Bastiano saw red and did not stay quiet. Instead, he gestured with his hand in the sign of horns and tossed Gino the biggest insult of all.

'Cornuto!'

Cuckold.

Bastiano, the villagers agreed, was the worst of the worst.

CHAPTER ONE

SOME NIGHTS WERE HELL.

'Bastiano!'

He heard the familiar, syrupy call of his name and knew that he must be dreaming, for Maria was long dead.

Unusually, he was alone in bed and as dawn sneaked over Rome, Bastiano fought to wake up.

'Bastiano!'

She called his name again.

When he reached his hand down and felt that he wasn't hard for her, it was a triumph, and Bastiano smiled a black smile as he silently told her she didn't do it for him any more.

Maria slapped his cheek.

She wore his mother's ring on her finger and he felt the cold metal as she delivered a stinging slap, one that had his hand move to his face for the wound was gaping. His cheek was sliced open and there was blood pouring between his fingers.

Bastiano fought with himself even in sleep. He knew that he was dreaming, for the savage fight with Raul had happened at the graveyard; the wound to his cheek had come *after* Maria had been lowered to the ground.

Everyone had said that it was Bastiano's fault she was dead.

And it was the reason that he was here, some fifteen years later—lying in one of the presidential suites at Rome's Grande Lucia hotel.

Raul Di Savo was considering its purchase, which meant that it had been placed on the top of Bastiano's must-have list.

Bastiano forced himself to wake up. He lay there in the darkness and glanced over at the hotel's bedside clock. Reaching over, he switched off the alarm. He had no need for it. He would not be going back to sleep.

Bastiano knew the reason that Maria was back in his dreams.

Well, she had never really left them, but that dream had been so vivid and he put it down to the fact that he and Raul were staying at the same hotel.

He heard the soft knock at the main door to his suite and then the quiet attempt to wheel in his breakfast trolley.

'Puzza!'

Bastiano smiled when he heard the small curse as the maid knocked into something and knew from that one word that the maid was Sicilian.

The door to the master bedroom had been left open but she quietly knocked again.

'Entra,' he said.

Bastiano was more than used to room service. Not only was he considering the purchase of this hotel but he was the owner of several premium establishments of his own. He closed his eyes, indicating, as she came in, that he wanted no conversation.

Sophie could see that he had made no move to sit up so she did not offer him a 'Good morning'.

The rules were very specific at the Grande Lucia and the staff were well trained.

Sophie loved her job, and though she did not usually do the breakfast deliveries she had been asked to do this one before her night shift ended. She had been called in to work late last night and so had missed the handover where the staff were told of any important guests, their idiosyncrasies and specific requests. Sophie, of course, knew that any guest staying in one of the presidential suites was an important one, and she had checked his name on his breakfast order.

Signor Bastiano Conti.

Being as quiet as she could, Sophie opened some heavy drapes and the shutters behind them so that the guest, when he sat up, would be greeted by the stunning view of Rome in all her morning glory.

And *what* a glorious day it was turning out to be!

It was as if the theatre curtains were opening on a beautifully set stage, Sophie thought.

There were a few clouds high in the sky that would soon burn off, for it was going to be a warm summer's day. The Colosseum was picture-postcard perfect and its ancient beauty gave her goosebumps.

Oh, it was a good day indeed for had she not made difficult choices and declined her family's desire for her to marry Luigi, today would have been the eve of her first wedding anniversary.

For a moment, Sophie forgot where she was and stood there simply taking in the view as she reflected on the past year. Yes, hard choices had been made but she was completely sure that they had been the right ones.

Oh, she was curious about men, of course she was, and though her mother would never understand it, she could readily separate that thought from marriage.

When she had tried to picture her wedding night and sleeping with Luigi, Sophie's blood had run cold. She had been out with a couple of younger men during her time in Rome but Luigi's wet, whiskery kisses had left their legacy and, though curious, Sophie had found herself ducking her head from any male advances.

Her parents imagined she was living a sinful life here in Rome.

Sadly, that couldn't be further from the truth!

Sophie was naïve, she knew that, but she was strong too.

Strong enough to say no to a man and a marriage she hadn't wanted.

'Buongiorno.'

A deep voice snapped her to attention and Sophie turned around as she realised that she had just been caught daydreaming, and by an important guest in his own suite!

She went to apologise but her flustered breath was literally taken away for there, lying in bed and idly watching her, was possibly a sight more arresting than the one she had just been feasting on. He was tall—she could see his length in the huge bed. His hands were behind his head and the sheet low on his stomach revealed his naked torso.

He really was magnificent, with olive skin and jet-black hair. The only blot on perfection was a jagged scar on his cheek, yet it only seemed to make him more beautiful. Most of all, it was his eyes that drew Sophie's. They were grey and piercing and as she met his gaze she found that her breath hitched in her chest and that she could not tear her gaze away. That was rare in itself for Sophie. In her job, she was very used to rich and beautiful men but with this one, with *this* one, she found that her eyes did not divert and, instead of an apology, her cheeks went a little bit pink.

'I was just preparing the view for you, Signor Conti,' Sophie said, and he gave a small smile in return as she made a little joke—as if she had been arranging the scenery outside specifically for him.

'Thank you.' He glanced towards the window and the million-euro view. 'You did a good job.'

And then he looked back at her.

When he had thought her to be taking her time Bastiano had opened his eyes to tell her to hurry up and leave, but there was something about her that halted his usual impatience.

And she mesmerised him now.

The eyes that met his were a very dark brown. He already knew from watching that she was as slender as a blade and wearing a pale green dress and flat shoes, both of which looked to be a little too big for her. Now he examined her face and saw that her thick black hair was worn up in a messy bun with a few long strands escaping.

She looked tired, Bastiano thought, and he guessed that her shift was just finishing rather than starting.

She had made him smile, just a little, but that was a surprise in itself given the dream he had so far failed to banish from his mind. The bedroom was rather messy and he was quite sure that the very sumptuous lounge was not much better; no doubt it was a stray bottle of champagne in the floor that had caused her small expletive on the way in.

'Would you like me to serve your breakfast?' she offered, still a little flustered and not just from being caught staring. Sophie made her way over to the breakfast trolley and lifted one of the silver domes.

'No, thank you,' Bastiano said. 'Actually, if you could bring me coffee that would be fine.'

'Would you like some water, or juice, too?' she offered, and then he saw the slight twitch to her lips and a certain knowing tone in her voice as she spoke on. 'Or perhaps you would like both?'

Again he smiled as she revealed her suspicions of his crashing hangover.

'Please.'

She brought over two glasses and Bastiano drank the cold water as she went back to the trolley and poured his coffee from the pot.

Usually Bastiano poured his own coffee for he did not like attempts at idle conversation, yet it was he who was pursuing it now.

'Sicilian?' he asked as she carried the cup to his bedside. She nodded and then, as she placed it on the table, she gave a little grimace, realising that he must have heard her swear.

'Me too,' he said calmly, and something in the delivery of his words told her that he got it, for the air was a touch bluer back home.

'What is that?' he asked, gesturing to the trolley, for despite the fact she had replaced the dome and covered the food there was now a rich, spicy scent mingling into the air.

'Shakshuka,' Sophie said. 'Middle Eastern baked eggs.'

The gorgeous guest screwed up his nose and Sophie was worried that the kitchen had got the orders mixed up so she quickly checked the paperwork on the trolley but, no, it was correct. 'You ordered it.'

'What was I thinking?' he drawled.

'I've heard that they're amazing,' Sophie said, and if the smell was anything to go by then her recommendation was bang on. 'Would you like me to take them back down and have something else sent to you?'

'It's fine.' He gave a shake of his head. 'Just leave it.'

'I hope you enjoy your day,' Sophie offered, and he gave a slight mirthless laugh and then nodded.

'You too.'

She went to close the bedroom door but he told her to leave it open.

As she left, Sophie picked up the bottle she had tripped over on her way in and put it on a tray. The room was a disaster and she would love, right this minute, to set about straightening things up, but it was not her job today and it was far too early to service a suite.

Anyway, as of now, she was off duty and so she headed to clock off and collect her things.

'What are you doing, delivering breakfasts?' Inga asked as Sophie retrieved her jacket from her locker. Just to be polite, Sophie had made a casual comment as to why she was a few minutes late coming off duty but Inga had, in her usual critical way, pounced. 'That is for the more senior chambermaids.'

'I just do as I'm told,' Sophie said, and poked her tongue out at Inga's departing back.

They did not get on.

Inga liked to deliver the breakfasts, especially to the very rich men, and though turning tricks was strictly forbidden, Sophie was quite certain that was the reason it was a designer bag that Inga had just put into her locker.

It wasn't for Sophie to judge and she tried not to.

Her dislike for Inga was simply due to the frequent disparaging comments and the endless digs that were sent her way. Sophie did her best to shrug them off but it was difficult at times. She didn't even know what she had done to incur Inga's wrath.

Still, she chose not to dwell on it. Sophie was more than ready for home—she was tired, hungry and ached for bed. Instead of heading out of the side entrance, Sophie, as she often did, decided to exit through the kitchen.

The reason was twofold.

It took her out to the alley, which was closer to the small flat she shared with two others.

And her little diversion would hopefully mean a free breakfast!

There were several chefs that worked in the kitchens, of course, but her favourite was Sicilian and he was just taking a batch of brioches out from the oven as she made her way over. Not the French brioche or even the sweet pastry those here in the north referred to; instead, these were the most delicious plain-baked buns of home. And he had made *millefoglie* too—also a bun, but with raisins mixed in and sugar on the top. Sophie guessed it was exactly the breakfast this morning's guest might wish that he had chosen.

Apart from Inga, Sophie was very well liked and popular at the Grande Lucia. She was a very good worker and always went the extra mile for guests. Signor Conti's mirthless laugh had stayed with her and so, instead of sneaking a brioche for her walk home, she spoke with the chef. He arranged a plate of freshly baked pastries and she put a small silver dome over it and then took her jacket off and, placing it over her arm, she headed back up to Signor Conti's suite.

She knocked and let herself in and then called out.

'Room service.'

After the maid had left, Bastiano had got up, taken one look at the eggs and replaced the dome.

His friend Alim, the current owner of the hotel, had always suggested he try them when they met for brunch and last night as he'd squinted at the selections it had seemed a good idea.

Not now.

There was no point him even being here.

Last night Alim had told him that his plans had suddenly changed and that he would not be able to show him through the hotel today as planned.

That wasn't all that irked Bastiano.

For once—in fact, for the first time in his life—a woman had turned him down.

In recent weeks, Bastiano had decided he would like a wife, and one with a castle in England and money problems had appeared to fit the bill.

It had seemed a decent solution at the time.

Lydia Hayward, with her breeding and porcelain looks would, he had decided, be the perfect trophy wife. It would be mutually beneficial, of course, and for his part he would help with her family's dire financial situation. He had flown her and her stepfather, Maurice, over to Rome so that he could kill two birds with one stone— view the hotel and put in an offer that would blow Raul out of the park. And maybe return home to Casta having secured a bride.

The more he had thought about it, the more he had decided that it might just be enough to rattle Raul—for Bastiano was more than financially secure, but settled... not so much.

But his plans hadn't exactly worked out that way.

Lydia had decided she would spend the evening catching up with friends and had left him hanging with the appalling Maurice.

Bastiano hadn't even attempted small talk with the man; instead, he had come back to his suite, and with his mood too dark to hit the clubs he had hit the bottle instead.

A foolish choice, in retrospect, for it had not been Lydia who had crept into his mind as he'd slept.

It had been Maria.

Fifteen years on and he could not fathom that he had ever cared for another person, for he cared for no one now.

No one.

Bastiano had a reputation for cold-hearted ruthlessness that ran from the boardroom to the bedroom.

Beating Raul Di Savo was the only thing that interested him.

He heard a knock at his door and a voice that was too cheerful for his black mood announce that room service was here.

Again!

Bastiano put a towel around his hips and walked out, more than ready to tell her to get the hell out and that, had he wanted a second delivery, he would have picked up the phone himself.

Yet she smiled so nicely as she took the lid from the plate she carried and held it out.

'Better?' she asked, as his eyes went to the plate.

Now, *that* was breakfast.

And his eyes went back to hers. No, they were not simply dark brown, they were the amber of a fox, and her smile was so bright that Bastiano could not bring himself to chide her. 'Much,' he rather reluctantly replied.

'I thought so too. Would you like another coffee?'

'That would be good.'

He got back into bed with the towel still round his hips and breakfast was served for the second time.

'You didn't have to do that,' Bastiano commented as, once in bed, she handed him the plate.

He guessed she must know that he was the potential new owner, for all the staff were walking on eggshells around him.

'I know.' She smiled 'But I also know that we have the best Sicilian chef here at the Grande Lucia. I was going to sneak a brioche for the walk home and it made me think of you.'

Perhaps she did not know that he might soon be the new owner? Bastiano could not care less about her sneaking a pastry. His staff all got meals on their shifts anyway, he made sure of that, but many owners were strict about such things.

'What's your name?'

'Sophie.' She saw him glance at the jacket over her arm. 'Really, it's not a problem—I am at the end of my shift.'

'Then would you like to stay and have some Middle Eastern eggs?' he offered, teasing her by replaying her words. 'I have been told that they're amazing.'

'No, thank you.' Sophie let out a small laugh as she shook her head. She wasn't unused to suggestions from businessmen and had declined her share over the last year. Sophie was no Inga!

'Enjoy.'

'I am.' He had torn open the brioche and as she left, the scent that reached him was the one of home and he spoke, really without thinking. 'I used to collect these from the bakery.'

'Ha!' Sophie said, turning around. 'Until I came to Rome I used to work at a bakery.'

'For how long?'

'Seven years,' Sophie said. 'Since I left school.'

And it was very easy—too easy—to speak of home. She missed it.

Oh, Sophie loved the life she had made here in Rome, but there was an ache for home at times, so for a moment they chatted, really just about the food and the stunning

Strait of Sicily. He guessed that she was also from the west. He was about to ask her exactly where but then Sophie yawned.

'Excuse me,' Sophie said. 'I really do have to go, all this talk of...' And she stopped because he had invited her to eat already and it might seem that she was angling for him to ask her again if she said just how hungry she felt.

Maybe she *was* angling?

Later she would look back and try to remember exactly how she had felt at that moment.

Happy and relaxed. It felt nice to be in his company.

'Have breakfast,' Bastiano said.

There was no motive.

That in itself was beyond rare for Bastiano, for he lived by motive, he did nothing without motive, yet all he saw this morning was that she was tired and probably hungry after a long shift.

And she heard, absolutely, the kindness in his offer and so, with just the briefest hesitation, she nodded.

'Thank you.'

Sophie could not know that kindness in Bastiano generally did not exist.

CHAPTER TWO

IT WAS AS natural as that.

The conversation between them came readily and it was simply pleasant to be with him. Sophie put her jacket on a chair and poured herself some chilled water and placed it on a tray. To that she added the plate of *shakshuka* and then looked around, wondering where she should take it to eat. First she glanced over at the chair where she had placed her jacket but it was rather full as his was there too. It was inside out so she could see the deep aubergine lining as well as a crumpled white shirt on the floor beside it. She looked at Bastiano, who was moving more to the centre of the bed, as if to make room for her to sit there, and so, instead of the chair, she made her way over to the bed.

Yes, it was as natural as that to walk over and sit on the edge of the huge bed, not too close, but alongside his thighs. She placed the tray on her lap.

The cloche had kept warm the eggs that were nestled in a rich-looking sauce, and she took her first tentative taste. It was a little spicier than expected and Sophie missed his smile as she reached for her water.

'Nice?' Bastiano asked.

She turned and looked at him and her eyes moved briefly to the scar on his cheek—Sophie would have loved to know its source—but then she looked back to his eyes. 'You know when you have wanted to try something for a very long time and then finally you do…'

Her words were not meant as provocative and they were not taken as such, for he was waiting for her to screw up her nose and to say that it was not as nice as she had thought it would be, but then she smiled. 'It is better than I expected.'

It was then that her words were provocative, though only to Sophie—for the pleasure of his company had her thoughts taking her mind to places they had never been.

He was stunningly attractive, yes, and she was no fool as to her situation, yet as Sophie looked at him her throat seemed to close in on itself and she could feel the pulse beat in her neck.

She was innocent from the lips down, and those lips had determinedly stayed as closed as they could when she had kissed her fiancé.

She had never shared a meal in a man's bedroom, or sat on a bed with a man and chatted so easily.

And neither had she ever stared so readily into another's eyes.

It truly was better than expected.

Was it the hot Baharat mix in the *shakshuka* that made her cheeks suddenly redden, or was it the first stirrings of desire?

Sophie did her best not to dwell on that thought. She tore her gaze from his and spoke on quickly. 'Apparently Sultan Alim has put a lot of new things on the menu since he took over the hotel.'

'Sultan?' Bastiano asked. He and Alim were friends. The Grande Lucia was Bastiano's favoured hotel when in Rome, and he and Alim often painted the town a rich shade of red but, despite lavish spending and wild ways, as far as Bastiano knew, Alim had always kept his royal status under wraps as best he could.

'We only found out that he was royal a few months ago,' Sophie revealed. 'His family came to stay and so of course the desk staff soon worked it out.' She thought for a moment. 'He's a good boss.'

'In what way?' Bastiano asked. He liked to hear the things that were important to staff, and knew that that sort of information could not readily be gleaned from a questionnaire or an appraisal. He didn't want to admit it, but he also just liked hearing her thoughts.

'He knows all of his staff by name,' Sophie said. 'And he is fair and kind. There was a Christmas meal and gift for all the staff who were working over the festive season.' She was silent for a moment as she thought back to that lonely day—coming to work had been the brightest part.

'How long have you worked here?' Bastiano asked.

'For nearly ten months. I've been in Rome for just over a year.' Sophie thought back to when she had first arrived and how nervous she had been, for she had never spent so much as a night away from home until then. 'It took a few weeks to find a job. I would have taken anything, but then I came for my interview and I wanted to work here so badly. I never thought I would get it as there was two months' training involved, but Benita took me on.'

'Benita?'

'The head of housekeeping,' Sophie explained. 'It is so much better than my old job.'

'I guess working at a bakery would have meant many early starts?'

'So early!' Sophie nodded and rolled her eyes. 'The shifts here are much better and the staff are really friendly. Well,' she added, thinking of Inga, 'most of them are.'

'Most?'

'There is always the odd person that you don't get on with in any workplace.' Sophie shrugged. 'I enjoy working here; I can't believe my luck really. It is, for me, the perfect job.'

'Why?'

'I like order,' Sophie said. 'I like things to be neat and tidy. When I see a suite such as yours, I itch to have it back as it should be.'

'Really?'

'Yes, really.' She nodded her head in the direction of the chair. 'I would have that jacket hanging up and that shirt put away.' Then she looked back at him. 'I would have that bed made, even with you in it...' And she hesitated. It was something that she often said as a joke to guests, usually the ones on the twelfth floor when she shooed them out to service their room.

It was not something that would ever be said to a guest such as Bastiano; he would never be shooed out, even jokingly.

It was not just that thought that had her pause, it was more a sudden awareness of their situation that silenced her.

Yet she had let the words out, and they were how she felt.

Not so much a neat bed, of course, more the thoughts that were there—an emerging awareness that made the room feel a little warmer.

Bastiano said nothing, just held her unblinking gaze until she spoke on.

'It really is the perfect job. Sometimes people ask me what I want to be, or they ask if I am working while studying, but I want only this—I'm happy now.'

'That's a very good place to be,' Bastiano said, though he couldn't fathom it for himself. The more he had the more he wanted, the more he achieved the further the goal seemed to stretch. 'Do you miss your family and friends?'

'I've made some friends...' She thought of her flat-mates and though they were not particularly close she got on well with them. And Sophie thought of Gabi, a wedding planner, who she had met on her first weekend here and had got on with straight away.

Usually Bastiano would leave it there. In fact, usually it would never have reached this point, for sitting in bed and chatting with a woman was not something Bastiano did regularly.

Regularly? Ha! Ever.

Yet he found he wanted to know her better.

'Do you miss home?' Bastiano asked, carefully re-wording his question.

'Sometimes,' she admitted. 'But if I was still there...' Sophie stopped what she was about to say and put down her cutlery, even though her meal was not finished. The conversation was edging towards topics that she usually kept closed.

Her newly made friends knew little about her. To them she was Sophie, twenty-four years old and happily single.

They had no idea how hard she had fought and how much she had given up to achieve such a small victory.

'*If* you were there?' Bastiano pushed, and now he *was* fishing—he really did want to know more about her.

She was about to stand, to end the conversation and get on with her day. Return to the real world.

Surprisingly, she found she liked this one.

Sophie liked the peace in his bedroom and the ease with which she spoke with this man.

She thought of his kind smile when she had realised he'd heard her swear. It had been a smile that had spoken of mutual understanding and a familiarity with the ways back home.

Something told her that he would…understand.

And though she had in the main been happy, it had also been a lonely twelve months.

'I was engaged to be married,' Sophie admitted. 'Had I stayed, tomorrow would have been my first wedding anniversary.'

'Had you stayed?' Bastiano verified. 'So it was you who ended it?'

'In a very mature and thoughtful way.' Sophie nodded and then she gave a small laugh that told him she was joking about handling things in an adult fashion. 'I ran away, if it is possible to run away from home when you are twenty-three. A month before the wedding I took a train to Rome and when I got here I called my parents and told them that I would not be marrying Luigi.'

He laughed at her explanation, although not un-kindly—it was a deep, low laugh that was almost enough reward in itself for that awful phone call she had made to her parents.

Something told Sophie that he did not laugh easily, that what was happening this morning between them was both delicious and rare.

And then that low laugh faded, like a roll of soft thunder moving through her.

Lightning had already struck, Sophie realised.

She was here alone in his room and it was exactly where she wanted to be.

'Have you been back home since?' he asked, seemingly unaware of the dance in her mind. Sophie was terribly grateful for the resumption of conversation, and answered hurriedly for her thoughts were all over the place.

'No, it was a big disgrace. I expected them to be cross but when it came to my birthday and my mother would not even come to the phone I realised just how bad things were.'

'When was your birthday?' he asked.

'A few months after I ran away.' She told him the date. 'It was pretty miserable.'

Birthdays had always been about family and standing around a cake while having a hundred photos taken.

Not this time.

It had been the same at Christmas—and the reason she had been so grateful that Alim ensured his staff celebrated also. Her flatmates had all gone home to be with their families and so the meal and gift from work had been the only Christmas that Sophie had had.

'They must miss you,' Bastiano said, but Sophie shook her head.

'I'm not sure that they do. I come from a big family; they wanted me married so that there would be one less. You know how things are back home.'

He nodded. Bastiano did know how things were for many but then he looked at Sophie and was still sure of one thing—they *must* miss her, because from the moment she had opened the drapes it had been as if an extra ray of sunshine had been let in. 'Will you go back?'

'I'm their only daughter...' She shrugged but it belied the pain behind the inevitable decision. 'If I return then I am to abide by their rules. I don't know what will happen. For now, though, I live my dream.'

Even if it was lonely at times.

'What about you?' she asked.

'I don't have any family.'

'None?'

He shook his head and he saw that she waited for him

to elaborate. 'I was raised by my mother's brother and his wife.'

'What about your mother?'

'She died.'

'How old were you?'

He didn't answer.

'What about your father?'

'You know as much about him as I do—nothing.'

'Not quite.' Sophie smiled. 'I know that he was good looking.'

Yes, she was like sunlight because until now, when he had revealed that his father was unknown, it had either terminated the conversation or resulted in averted eyes or a derisive comment. Not with Sophie, for she turned the awkwardness around as she smiled—and possibly flirted—and the conversation was far from closed.

'What happened with your *zia* and *zio*?' she asked.

'I see them on occasion but we don't really speak,' Bastiano said, peeling off some brioche and handing it to her to mop up the last of the spicy sauce. 'They threw me out when I was seventeen.' He thought of the row they had had after the affair had been exposed and it had come to light that he had slept with the enemy—a Di Savo. 'Deservedly so.'

'So what are you doing here in Rome?' Sophie asked. 'Business?'

'In part,' Bastiano said, but knew that he was being evasive. Sophie obviously had no clue that he was considering purchasing the hotel. He didn't want to enlighten her for he knew that it would put a wedge between them. So to avoid speaking of work he told her something rather personal. 'I got dumped last night.'

'Oh!' She smiled at his revelation. 'I cannot imagine anyone dumping you.'

'Neither could my ego,' Bastiano admitted, and then he told her a bit more. 'She's English and lives in a castle.'

'Nice,' Sophie said, and he shrugged.

'It would have been a lot of work.'

Sophie frowned, not sure what he meant by that.

'What was your fiancé like?' he asked, curious about the man she had left behind.

'He was a lot older than me, more than forty years old,' Sophie said, and screwed up her face.

'Is that why you ended it?'

'Not really.' She shook her head. Looking back at that time, she remembered that moment when she had felt as if she could see her life spreading out before her, and not liking what she saw.

Sophie had never discussed it with anyone and perhaps she should not now but there was nothing regular about this morning. She had never met anyone who felt less like a stranger before. Bastiano knew more about her than her flatmates and she had lived with them for a year. More about her than Gabi, for she had been a touch elusive of late and their catch-ups had petered out. And he knew more about her than her parents, for they had never once asked for her take on things.

'Luigi came over to my parents' for dinner, as he often did…'

Bastiano said nothing, he even fought a slight eye rise, but at forty shouldn't the guy have at least been entertaining her?

Sophie glanced at him—the truth was a touch personal, but his eyes were patient and finally there was a person to whom she could speak her truth.

'That night I felt a little sick and didn't really eat much. When my mother took away the plates and my brothers and father left us alone he asked what was wrong with me. I told him that I had gone on the Pill.' She blushed just a little as she said it but far less than she had when she had told her fiancé. In fact, Bastiano seemed completely at ease with the sensitive topic.

Unlike Luigi.

It hadn't been up for discussion. Sophie had had to find everything out for herself. Even the village doctor hadn't been particularly friendly. In the end, it had been her friend at the bakery who had told her that she could skip her period entirely if she chose.

'What was his reaction?' Bastiano asked.

'He seemed cross. He said, "Why would you go on that?" Then he told me that he wanted children straight away and a lot of them!'

She pulled such a horrified face that Bastiano laughed.

And there was that thunder again, only this time she was counting the minutes, for the delicious storm drew closer with each revelation and with each passing word.

'I said that we needed my wage from the bakery and my mother came in from the kitchen. She didn't hear the part about the Pill, of course, just me saying I would put off having children so I could work, and she said she would look after them. It's not that I don't want children...'

He halted her when she tried to further explain for there was no need.

'Sophie,' he said in that rich voice of his, 'well done for running away.'

Bastiano was the first person she had really told about it and his reaction made her feel warm with pride for her choice, rather than sick with shame as her family had.

'Thank you.'

Oh, they were as natural as that, for Bastiano, who rarely bothered with conversation, was telling her some more about himself.

'I flew Lydia over from England with her stepfather, Maurice, under the guise of business. We were supposed to be meeting in the bar and then going out for dinner but when she turned up she said that she was going out with friends instead.'

Sophie gave him a quizzical look, because she really couldn't imagine declining dinner with him, but Bastiano read her frown as curiosity.

'I think she had worked out it wasn't just dinner.' He saw her cheeks darken in a blush and he further clarified that it had not been sex he was after. Bastiano had no trouble at all finding that. 'Like your fiancé, I had got it into my head that maybe it was time to settle down.'

Though his main reason had been simply to beat Raul to it.

Bastiano had everything money could buy and so too did Raul. The only thing neither had was a family.

He had decided that he would be first.

It had been as simple as that.

'Had you been going out with each other for long?' Sophie asked.

'We'd never been out.' Bastiano yawned and it really was a relief not to have to explain that romance and love were not always prerequisites for marriage back home. 'It just seemed like a good idea at the time, though not so much now.' He shrugged. 'Easy come, easy go. On reflection, I think I'm far more suited to the single life.'

'Well, with your looks and...' she looked around the lavish suite and stated the obvious '...your money, why not have fun?'

'Oh, I do,' Bastiano said.

Though lately he wouldn't describe it as fun.

He lay back on the pillow, but as their eyes met the silence was heavy. She wore no make-up, not a scrap, Bastiano noted as he took in her dark lashes. He felt her gaze move to his mouth and for once he was unsure where they were going, for usually when a woman was on his bed there was no question as to what was about to happen.

Come here, he wanted to say.

Sophie knew that.

Her perfect storm had now gathered and it would be so terribly easy to be swept into it, but she really was no Inga, even if he perhaps thought of her as such.

There was a reason the maids were told not to accept gifts.

Yet there was no air of expectancy from Bastiano.

Sophie felt no pressure as she put down her cutlery, took a drink of water and then stood.

She gave him a polite smile and effortlessly she was back to being a maid. She put her plate neatly back on the trolley.

'Thank you,' Sophie said. 'That was delicious.'

'You're more than welcome,' Bastiano said. 'So were the pastries.'

She came over to collect his plate.

It rested on his thigh and, though covered by the sheet, Sophie thought it was better that he be the one to retrieve it for she could see a black snake of hair on his stomach—as much as she tried not to look. There was desire pitted low in her stomach and an itch to pull the sheet down. Her hands shook a little and just like that she was no longer a maid. Their fingers met for a little too long and rather than pull back she lingered for his skin was warm and even that slight touch had her aching for more.

'I have to go,' she said as she fought for control.

'Of course.'

Yet still she stood there and instead of turning away

she put the plate down on the bedside table. She was not so much uncertain, more nervous of her own curiosity.

'Thank you,' she said again.

Bastiano could not read her, for he could feel her desire and yet sense her reticence so he moved things along a fraction. His index finger came up and he tapped it twice on the cheek nearest to her, the one that was not scarred.

A kiss to the cheek was still okay, Sophie thought, for she would kiss her friend Gabi on the cheek when they said farewell after sharing a meal. But even as she tried to convince herself, Sophie knew that this situation was nowhere near as innocent as that.

It wasn't even a conscious decision. It was more that she might as well have been standing on a conveyer belt, for it was as if she glided towards him.

She bent forward and moved her mouth to where his finger had tapped, the place where his rough morning shadow transitioned into smooth skin. The contrast sent shivers down her spine. The warmth of him on her lips was enticing and her tongue fought not to taste as her lips lingered.

Sophie sensed him holding his breath and hers now came a little too fast in response. She pulled her head back and moved to kiss the other cheek.

Bastiano jerked his head a little, for he did not like anyone touching his scar. He would by far prefer her mouth to meet his and usually he got what he wanted.

Not this time.

She misread the small signal and her mouth moved to his other cheek. Once on his scar, her lips lingered there, kissing him softly as if she didn't care about the damage beneath.

CHAPTER THREE

THERE WAS A gap between their chests, but so in tune was Sophie with his every move that she felt as if their bodies touched.

It was time to stay or go, Sophie knew. Even at this stage she could smooth it over and make her farewells.

Or she could meet those lips and discover bliss.

With Luigi, she had dreaded a kiss, let alone sex.

Not now.

When she had left home at twenty-three, Sophie had been considered a disgrace for her failure to commit.

She was twenty-four now and there was no disgrace to be had here.

It was better than her dreams. And so much better than the reality she had run from.

'Come here,' he moaned, and his hand came up and pulled her head down onto his.

Always she had avoided such contact, yet now she craved it.

His mouth was soft, and the dark shadow of his skin did not make her skin crawl with its tickle; instead, it was rough and delicious and matched the building desire in her.

Now, instead of resisting, she opened her lips, wanting and willing.

His tongue felt like a reward as it coiled around hers,

and then he slowly suckled the tip. They tasted each other, and they inflamed each other and not just with their mouths. He was stroking her breast through the fabric of her dress. His thumb was teasing her nipple and Sophie ached for bed.

His bed.

She pulled back, and knew that even now she could walk out having shared no more than a kiss.

'You taste spicy,' Bastiano said.

'And you taste sweet.'

'But I'm not,' he warned her.

'I'm working,' she told him, for she would get into the most terrible trouble if anyone found out.

'You finished an hour ago,' he reminded her, and then he stretched out an arm and she heard the click of a button that would turn on the Do Not Disturb sign outside.

'I'm in my uniform…'

'Good,' he said.

He thought her experienced, Sophie suspected.

Perhaps now would be the time to tell him she was not. That this morning was, in fact, a most irregular occurrence for her.

But Sophie knew that would change things. And there was nothing about this man and this morning she would change, even if she could.

Sophie wondered if she was on that conveyer belt again, for she moved so easily to be closer to him and when he guided her so that she sat on his stomach, she went readily.

Bastiano looked up as his fingers undid the buttons to her uniform and revealed a threadbare bra so sheer that her nipples could almost part the fabric and he could see the dark of her areolae. His hands cupped her breasts and he wanted her to shrug off the dress, to discard the bra and to lower her head, yet she closed her eyes in bliss as he toyed with her breasts.

'Take down your hair,' he told her, for he wanted the curtain between them when she took him in her mouth; he guided her back so that she sat on his thighs and the sheet moved with her.

She saw him erect, and since it was the first time she had seen, let alone touched, such a thing she held him in her hands.

'Sophie,' he said, for he did not want hands and tentative fingers even as he grew to them.

He was mesmerised, though, watching as she stroked.

Simply touching him was compelling. The feel of soft skin was a contrast to the strength in her palm and there was a coil of want that seemed to tighten within him as she gripped him more firmly.

'Take down your hair,' he said again, yet Sophie did not care for his orders, for the pleasure that grew was not just his. Her knickers were damp and she ached to feel him there. She wanted to stand and remove them, yet her legs felt clamped to his thighs.

She ran a finger over the tip and teased out a silver drop; the moan he gave had her rise to her knees.

He lifted the skirt of her dress, taking his own thick length and running it over her covered mound.

Sophie knelt up with her hands on his chest, biting on her lip at the exquisite pleasure he delivered. Oh, it was wrong! If she examined it, then she knew that was the only conclusion that could be drawn.

Yet there was so much that she had not even known was missing and she felt like a colourblind person able to see a rainbow for the first time.

She had for a long time dreaded sex and that dread had now completely gone. Sophie was turned on like she had never been in her life. Even in her imaginings there had never been desire such as this.

Despite the barrier of fabric he pushed in just a little way, enough to incite and make her ache for more.

He reached into the bedside drawer for condoms while she hovered and teased, and then he held a condom out for her once she had peeled off her knickers.

'Put it on,' he said, his voice ragged as his fingers met the pink lips that would soon enclose his length. 'Sophie…' His impatience was building for he had to be inside her. 'Put it on.'

And then she spoke and the words that she said stilled him.

'I don't know how.'

Bastiano's conscience had left him a long time ago.

He had thought it buried alongside Maria, for he cared nothing for anyone, but when it hit that he would be her first, his conscience made itself known once more.

Bastiano knew very well how things worked, especially in hotels, and often he didn't need to go out or even pick up the phone for sex to drop into his lap.

Sophie wasn't his usual style—an innocent conversation and a breakfast.

Sophie really was sweet.

'What the hell are you doing here, then?' he asked.

'The same as you,' she told him, and his lips pressed together as he got first hand a taste of her defiant streak.

'I think you should go.' His conscience seemed to stand in the wings and, like a prompter, told him the words he should say. 'I'm not looking to get involved with anyone. I'm back to the single life, Sophie.'

'You already told me that,' she said.

'You've been saving yourself, and a one-night stand in a hotel room—'

'It's morning,' Sophie interrupted, but Bastiano was having none of it and he tipped her from his lap and pulled up the sheet.

'Go.'

There was no air of negotiation to his tone but still she sat there.

'Out,' he told her, and Sophie climbed from the bed.

Humiliated, she stuffed her knickers into her uniform pocket as Bastiano looked at the ceiling, or rather anywhere than at Sophie.

And again she could see her life spreading out before her.

Regret.

Utter regret that her first time had not been with someone as beautiful and sensual as him.

She was twenty-four and she ached to know such intimacies.

Bastiano was exquisite.

He was male beauty personified, expensive yet raw too, with a visceral undercurrent that finally matched hers.

That was why she had waited—to find someone who was her match.

Maybe later she would finally give in to her parents' silent demands and return home. Perhaps someday she would settle and marry and pretend that it was her first time, while holding the secret that it had been him all along.

Almost.

'You're right,' she said, and went to do up some of the buttons on her uniform. 'I *have* been saving myself—for a time and a person of my choosing.'

'You can do better.'

'Please...' she scoffed.

Now he looked from the ceiling and at her as Sophie spoke.

'This time last year I was told I could do no better than the man they had lined up to take my virginity.'

'But he would have been your husband.'

'Do you think it helped to know that?' she asked, and her question was both important and urgent.

'No,' Bastiano admitted, and there was a flicker of guilt that flared because of his own quest for a trophy wife. He looked at Sophie, still doing up her uniform; in the bedroom he usually didn't need to think, yet she was clever and strong and knew her own desires.

'It doesn't matter,' Sophie said. She was starting to think of all the professional consequences of this current humiliation. He was, after all, a guest, and she was desperately trying to get back to being a maid. 'I am sorry for any misunderstanding…'

Bastiano loathed her apology.

There had been no misunderstanding.

'Sophie.'

She ignored him and headed for the bedroom door. This time she would not be returning. Her cheeks were on fire and, rarely for Sophie, she felt on the edge of tears.

He was doing her a favour, Bastiano told himself.

Yet it was a favour that neither of them wanted.

'Sophie.' This time he said it as he got out of bed.

Bastiano had never run after anyone but he called her name again just as she walked through the door. Sophie paused and turned around.

He was entirely naked; he hadn't even attempted to bring the sheet with him. The sight of him standing naked caused her to breathe as if she had taken the stairs all the way up to his suite.

He was tall, so tall that as he stood right in front of her

she was at eye level between his clavicle and one dark mahogany nipple.

'You forgot your jacket.'

She didn't look up and neither did she look down; the chair near the window seemed like a very long way away. 'Could you fetch it for me, please?'

'Are you sure?' His hand came to her chin and gently but firmly he forced her head up so that she looked at him.

'I don't understand the question.'

'Yes, you do.' For his words had nothing to do with the jacket that lay over the chair, and they both knew it. Still, he clarified. 'Sophie, I leave tomorrow morning. Maybe we could have dinner tonight…?'

And that in itself was a concession by his standards, for it was usually dinner and then bed, rather than the other way around.

Yet with his hands holding her chin she shook her head and surprised herself when she did, in fact, turn down dinner with this stunning man. 'I'm working tonight.'

And so he asked her again. 'Are you sure this is what you want?'

Not once in her lifetime had she been so certain. She wanted this man.

Decisions had all too often been made by others on her behalf.

From the friends she kept to the clothes she wore.

On her thirteenth birthday she had said that she would like to go shopping for clothes. There was a skirt she had seen and a top too, and instead she had come home from school to be told there was a surprise for her in the bedroom.

On her bed lay a new dress and sandals.

They were pretty enough, though best suited to a ten-year-old and not what she would have chosen. Even Sophie had not fully understood the disappointment and even anger that had welled inside her as she had thanked her smiling parents.

And she could well remember being told that it was time to leave school as her father had found her a job at the baker's.

And though she had smiled and worked hard and been proud to bring home a wage to help take the pressure from her family, she had always felt as if she were somehow not living her own life.

Being told that it was time to marry had proved to be the final straw for Sophie.

"He's twenty years older than me," she had said when they had told her whom she would marry.

"Then he's steady," her mother had replied. "Reliable."

The man Sophie looked at now was none of those things, yet Bastiano had not only asked if she was sure this was what she wanted, he had paused to have her confirm it.

It was indeed potent to be asked.

For once the choice was hers.

And so she made it. She would have him.

'Very.'

CHAPTER FOUR

IT WAS BASTIANO who closed the shutters and then the drapes and turned on the bedside lights.

The breakfast trolley he pushed out of the bedroom then he closed the door.

She had expected a fierce kiss, and to resume where they had left off, but Bastiano had decided that this should not be rushed.

'Are you nervous?' he asked, walking over to her.

'No,' Sophie said.

Her response was unexpected but, then, so was everything about this morning, Bastiano thought.

'Not at all?' he checked, for he could see the pulse leap in her throat as he stood in front of her and, more slowly this time, started to undo the buttons.

'I get nervous when I call my parents.' She smiled at his serious face and moved her own closer to his. 'And I get nervous when I go to pay for my groceries because I am not sure if I have enough money to cover...'

He smiled and she moved in and stole a kiss from his cheek, a kiss that moved to his ear. 'I don't feel like that now.'

He moved the dress down over her shoulders and watched it fall to the floor. Then he walked behind her and she felt his fingers unclasp her bra. Her knickers she had dispensed with earlier, and this was all that was left before they were naked together. His hands were warm over her arms as he moved the straps down slowly and then removed the flimsy garment.

He made her feel dizzy, her eyes closing as he ran a finger the length of her naked spine.

Now he turned her around and it felt as if every pore pleaded for his touch, for it was like being painted with fire as his eyes roamed her body.

'I feel like I know you,' she told him.

It made no logical sense for they had never so much as met before, yet she was not even close to feeling shy, and when he lifted his eyes to hers he made no promise with his reply.

'No one could.'

He led her to his bed and it was very different from before, for he gave no instructions. There was no point because Sophie would not follow them—that much he already knew.

'Aren't you going to ask me to take down my hair?' Sophie asked as she climbed between the sheets.

'No,' Bastiano said, for now he wanted no curtain between them.

Still she did not get the fierce welcome of his kiss; instead, she sank into a mattress that felt like a cloud and sheets and a pillow that were still a little warm from his body.

He lay on his side, propped up on one arm and looking down at her.

'Nice?' he asked as she closed her eyes in bliss.

'So nice.'

And so was the light touch of his hand on her breast. Less than a tickle and more than a brush, it made her breathe in sharply through her nostrils. His face came over hers and the kisses she had stolen as he had undressed her Bastiano now returned.

Each time his mouth met hers it was like a teasing glimpse of summer: warmth on her skin and the bliss of more to come, then the cool tease of distance.

The light touch of his fingers had her nipples harden like studs and he could read the need that spread through her. Each slip of his tongue coiled her tighter and the heat from his palm on her breast was a gentle torment. As his fingers squeezed her nipple hard she moaned, and was rewarded with a kiss.

So focused was she on the bliss that his lips delivered, she had barely registered the downward movement of his hand until it slipped between her thighs; he adored that they did not tighten but instead parted softly.

She tasted of all that was good, and he of all that was illicit.

His mouth moved down to her neck and the kiss on her tender skin at first was gentle but as skilled lips moved down his kisses deepened.

Sophie's hand pressed into his shoulder, feeling his warm skin as his mouth sought her breast. There he toyed, slowly at first, licking and teasing her nipple with his tongue. The scratch of his jaw was sublime and Sophie found her fingers digging into his shoulder when he sucked deeply.

Bastiano heard her soft moans, and he wanted to hear more of them so his fingers explored and pushed inside her.

She felt as if every nerve in her body was on fire with the source at her centre, as if she might fold over if he did not stop or that she would surely die if he did not go on. His mouth came back to hers and now his kiss was fierce as he teased and stroked her below.

She arched to his palm, her mouth opening wide, her jaw tensing as Sophie lost contact with the earth.

Bastiano wanted to kiss her all over and savour slowly each inch of skin, but feeling her beneath his fingers, slick and pouting, he felt himself driving closer to the point where he would be neither slow nor tender.

He reached for a condom, as he had before, but her words halted him. 'I'm still on the Pill.'

Bastiano would lecture her later, he decided. He knew he was safe, for he always wore protection—he trusted no one.

It was a first for them both, for he had never made love without one.

Not once.

There was slight trepidation in Sophie as his weight came over her, but it was quickly overridden by yearning.

'Nervous?' he checked.

'Never.'

Bastiano was.

The emotion caught him by surprise as he looked down into amber eyes, for she was so willing and wanting and he was so loath to hurt her.

For some reason he could not readily define, there was rare caution in him as he entered her a little way, and though he met resistance there was a warm willingness swallowing him in.

No, Bastiano did not rob Sophie of her innocence; she gladly relinquished it as she embraced the sensation of pain edged with bliss.

He moved up on his elbows and kissed her tense lips, fighting his own need.

Sophie squeezed her eyes closed for each slow movement from Bastiano delivered fresh trauma and her hand moved to his chest. It was a silent plea to take his time, but as he drew back the ache turned to need and her hips rose to him as he filled her again.

'Slowly,' she whispered, and she watched the tension in his features as he did his level best to honour that request.

She could feel him fight to keep the delicious, unhurried paced she demanded. And when the pain had left, when each stroke had her frenzied and thick desire filled her loins, Sophie removed her hands from his chest, ready to meet his fierce need to possess.

Their rhythm was intense, and he looked her right in the eyes. Her hands moved down his back to his taut buttocks as Bastiano dictated the pace.

He took her leg and wrapped it around him, positioning himself carefully with a patience her body could not return.

'Bastiano...' Sophie was suddenly frantic, her head slipping between huge pillows, but Bastiano flicked them away and rescued her head with his hand; he held her taut body, and only as she started to come did he cease his restraint and give her a glimpse.

Just a glimpse of Bastiano unleashed, but it was enough to harness the energy that built within; the ripple of her orgasm deepened and she shuddered as it swept fast through her.

In the throes of her cry, he knelt and thrust in deeper, his muscled arm scooping behind her back and lifting her body. Taking her hard, she was utterly open to him.

Sophie did not know where it ended, but she knew she came again to the final bucks of his desire.

He was looking down at the point of their joining, delivering those last precious drops deep within as she pulsed to him.

And it faded, for it had to.

As he released her, as he withdrew, Sophie knew that Bastiano had given her everything she could have wanted for her first time. He had taken care and brought her pleasure, he had opened her mind to her body, and it was in those dying seconds that she felt robbed.

Not of her virginity—she had been more than willing in that.

But of time.

There was so much more to Bastiano that she now ached to see.

CHAPTER FIVE

SOPHIE AWOKE MIDAFTERNOON, wrapped in Bastiano's arms.

If bliss was a place, then she had found it.

She lay there examining her needs and wants, only to find she was entirely content.

Oh, she needed the loo, but apart from that there was nothing, not a single thing she required. Sophie did not want to get up because she did not want to wake him, and because she did not want reality to impinge just yet.

Today, she decided, was her day and she intended to make it last!

She wriggled out of his arms, picked up her uniform and underwear and headed into the bathroom. It was sumptuous indeed, themed like a Roman bath with stone walls and a deep alabaster soaking tub that took centre stage. The windows were designed so that the guests could lie in splendour and gaze out on Rome with their privacy assured.

Only Sophie wasn't here for that—lazy days spent lying in an alabaster bath were not for the likes of her.

Turning on the tap and with a somewhat mischievous smile she threw her clothes in the sink. Not just to be sure that her uniform would be fresh for tonight but to make certain she would not be leaving any time soon!

Then she looked again at the bath that seemed to beckon and asked herself, Why not?

At her flat there was a small shower, and more often than not a flatmate waiting their turn.

Sophie knew she would never get a chance like this again.

And so, once she had hung her clothes over the towel warmers, rather than clean the bath, as Sophie so often did when she serviced a suite, instead she ran the deepest one and added everything that she possibly could to it—oils, salts, bubbles. All the lovely bottles that she usually replaced each day were now tipped into the steaming, fragrant water and then she climbed in herself.

This, she decided as the warm water engulfed her, was indulgence at its finest. As she lay there feeling utterly pampered, and with a body sated by his touch, Sophie knew that she would never look at this view again and not think of this wonderful day.

And that was how he had made her feel—simply wonderful.

There was no guilt about this morning's events, though perhaps that would come.

Had she done the right thing by her family's standard, her first time would have been a year ago and it would have been something to forget rather than remember. This was how it was supposed to feel, she knew that now.

She lay there and smiled, and closed her eyes to picture Bastiano better.

And that was how he found her when he came in, up to her neck in bubbles and half dozing.

'Why are there clothes hanging everywhere?' he asked. 'It looks as if the gypsies have arrived.'

Sophie opened her eyes and smiled, for he stood there

gorgeous and naked, frowning at her dripping uniform and underwear.

'If you must know, I washed them because you are a gentleman and I know that you would not send me out in wet clothes.'

'I admire your cunning,' Bastiano said. 'However, I am not a gentleman and if I wanted you gone then, wet clothes or not, you would be.'

'Nope.' She did not believe it of him, for in Sophie's eyes he was perfect.

She held out her hand for him to join her, but he hesitated because he generally didn't really care for such tender intimacies. He told himself that it was the fragrant, foaming water that seemed so inviting before climbing in at the opposite end, with his back to the view. Sophie rested her feet on his chest.

Certainly, Bastiano thought, if he did get into the bath with a woman then it was not to lie there half dozing, but that's exactly what he found himself doing.

For a while, at least.

But then her heels pressed into the wall of his chest.

He ignored her.

'What?' he asked, when her heels nudged him again.

'Rub them.'

He was too relaxed to decline, and so he got right into the soles with his thumbs, enjoying her moans of pleasure.

'Your posh English girl does not know what she's missing,' Sophie said.

She assumed him the kindest, most thoughtful person, Bastiano realised, and he chose not to enlighten her.

'Are you sore?' he asked, not meaning her feet.

'A little bit,' Sophie admitted, and then her lips twitched

provocatively as she met his eyes. 'Though not sore enough not to do it all again.'

Yes, Sophie decided, Lydia really did not know what she was missing because Bastiano massaged her calves as if he knew how they ached, and he made her feel as if there was nowhere else he wished to be.

'For skinny legs,' Bastiano said, 'you have a lot of muscle.'

'Because I am on my feet all day, climbing stairs.'

Not today, though.

Sophie accepted that they only had this day, but for the times ahead when she thought about these precious moments and her mind drifted to this intriguing man, there were things she would want to know.

And she was curious enough to ask.

'What happened to your cheek?'

It was rare that he was relaxed enough with anyone to answer.

'I got into a fight.'

'How old were you?'

'Seventeen.'

'Was the fight with your uncle?' she asked, because he had told her it was at that age he had been kicked out.

'No.'

'Seventeen was a busy year for you, then!'

'I guess.'

'Who was the fight with?' Sophie asked, and she ignored the warning in his eyes to leave it because she was too immersed in the sensual feel of his hands, though they stopped working her calves as he answered her.

'A man I hate to this day.'

Sophie looked over at the change to his tone. It did not unnerve her in the least; she just waited for him to go on, yet Bastiano revealed no more.

Always that type of conversation was marked out of bounds, yet he had opened up a touch and he found himself curious about her.

'What were you doing at seventeen?' he asked.

'I told you, I was working at the bakery...' And then she thought back to that time and she let out a small laugh. 'I was in love. Or at least I thought I was.'

'With whom?'

'A man who used to stop in on his way to work.'

'Did he stop by to see you?' Bastiano asked, assuming that to be the obvious case. 'I'd have been stopping by morning and night and again for cake at lunchtime.'

'Ah, but then you'd have become as fat as the baker.'

'I'd have worked it off,' Bastiano said, taking her legs and pulling her closer so that they both sat up and her legs wrapped around him. Together, they made an alternative reality where it *had* been Bastiano who'd stopped by in the mornings, and between teasing kisses she told him how it had been.

'It was nothing like that. He was married! I just had a crush and he very politely ignored it.'

And Bastiano wondered what her reaction would be if he told her his sins. Not that he had any intention of doing so.

She lay back down and closed her eyes, looking utterly at ease, as if she had not a care in the world.

Sophie didn't.

Not a single care.

'Usually I am cleaning this bath,' she sighed. 'Once I had to bring into this very bathroom a bucket of ice and its stand along with a bottle of champagne. That in itself is not uncommon, but on this occasion the couple were sitting in the bath.'

'Well, it wasn't me,' Bastiano said, his response dry.

'Of course not, you are too polite for that.'

He was about to correct her and say he really didn't give a lot of thought to sparing the maids' blushes—more that he tended not to indulge in romantic baths.

Yet here he was.

'What else have you seen?' he asked.

'So much.' Sophie smiled and leant back on the head-rest, closing her eyes as she recounted. 'There are lots of weddings here and I enjoy them the most. There is always something wonderful going on. I don't often deliver the breakfasts, but some mornings I do, and some couples have champagne at seven a.m....' She had questioned it the first time, but now she smiled at the romance of it. 'I've seen so many different sides to life, working here. I've never even tried champagne, let alone first thing in the morning.'

'Would you like me to call for some?' he offered.

'No,' Sophie said with her eyes still closed but then, as she had done when waking in his arms, she examined her wants. There were no needs—they had been more than taken care of—but there *was* a tiny want. 'I thought I wasn't hungry,' she said.

'And are you?'

'Not really,' Sophie admitted, but she was determined to make use of the good life while she had it. 'But I could *just* manage a gelato with a shot of hot espresso...'

He groaned as another of life's simple pleasures now became a necessity and Bastiano reached out for the bath-side phone. He gave his order, telling them they could override the Do Not Disturb sign on this occasion and leave the dish in the entrance to the suite.

Ten minutes later, Sophie lay in the bath with her hand clapped over her mouth, trying not to laugh as Inga wheeled their treats through to the lounge.

Bastiano was in a towelling robe and he didn't even close the doors so his conversation with Inga drifted through from the lounge and Sophie could hear every word that was said.

'Is there anything else I can do for you, Signor Conti?' Inga asked, and Sophie knew that she was not speaking out of turn because the suite looked as if they had visiting rock stars *in situ* and was in serious need of a full service.

'That is all,' Bastiano responded.

He came back into the bathroom and Sophie screwed up her nose. 'I cannot stand her,' she admitted.

'Why?'

'Just…' Sophie shrugged, suddenly a little awkward, for after all, wasn't she doing the same as Inga?

No, she decided, for this had nothing to do with money or designer bags. Instead, it was a promise that she had made to herself long ago—that her first time would be because she wanted it and was ready for it—and that promise to herself had been fulfilled. Still, Inga and thoughts of home were soon forgotten when she realised that he had come into the bathroom empty handed.

'Where's my gelato?'

He didn't answer. Instead, Bastiano came over and lifted her out of the bath, carrying her dripping wet back to the bed. She laughed and protested and he found himself smiling as he dropped her onto the bed.

'Here.' He propped her up on the pillows and poured a shot of hot coffee over the gelato and then handed her the dish. Sophie had a taste and gave a purr of pleasure. It was deliciously cold after the warm bath and the flavour, both sweet and bitter, was perfection.

She looked over as Bastiano took off his robe and then picked up his own dish but he did not add the espresso.

'Where's your coffee?' she asked.

'I don't think you'd like it,' Bastiano said, and then took a large scoop of ice cream and held it in his mouth, so that his tongue and lips were almost blue with cold.

'What are you doing?' Sophie asked as he knelt on the bed and parted her legs.

'Kissing it better.'

Yes, she had found bliss.

It was a day in bed spent hidden from the world.

A day spent making love, dozing, laughing and talking, and Sophie never wanted it to end, though of course she knew that it must.

Wrapped in his arms, Sophie woke and did not want to look at the bedside clock.

The drapes and shutters were heavy enough to block out every chink of light, but there was a certain stillness to the air and she knew that it was night.

Sure enough, when she lifted her head from Bastiano's chest and read the time, she saw that in less than an hour her shift would commence.

And they would end.

She slid out of his arms and went back to the gorgeous bathroom. This time she had a shower and then did up her hair and dressed in her dry clothes.

She walked back into the master bedroom and there lay Bastiano, asleep.

No, she would never regret it.

She had heard her friends speak of their first time and some of them had sounded dismal, some had been described as good at best.

This had been perfection. He had taken such care of her, both in and out of bed.

For the first time in her life she had been spoiled and

adored but she knew that the world they had built this day had not been one designed to last.

Sophie ached to wake him, but she did not know how to say goodbye without tears and that certainly wasn't a part of the deal they had made.

And so, instead of waking him, instead of fumbling through a goodbye that she did not want, Sophie went to the bureau in the lounge, took out a piece of paper and wrote him a little note.

Mai ti dimentichero' mai.

I will never forget you.

And if it was too sentimental for Bastiano, she didn't care, for she never would forget, Sophie thought as she quietly let herself out of the suite. Though sad to leave, as she headed to the elevator and awaited its arrival, there was the complete absence of guilt.

Her mother, if she knew, would never forgive her and that was no idle thought—it was fact. And neither would Benita, the head of housekeeping, if she were ever to find out.

Yes, to others it might seem wrong, but to Sophie everything felt right with the world and she hugged the memory of them close to her chest.

It had been the best day of her life without a doubt, and if it were possible to float in an elevator, then that was just what Sophie would have done as she made her way down to the foyer.

She actually didn't start work for another ten minutes but knew that her friend Gabi was working on the plans for a wedding being held tomorrow.

No, she wouldn't tell even Gabi about what had happened—some things were too precious to share. But she couldn't find her friend; Sophie put her head around the ballroom doors and saw that she wasn't there.

In fact, there was no sign of her.

It felt as if Gabi might be avoiding her because usually they caught up all the time, but for the past couple of months Gabi had always been too busy or tired.

Sophie headed through the foyer and to Reception, where Anya was on duty.

'Have you seen Gabi?' she asked.

'Gabi!' Anya said, and gave a dramatic eye-roll. 'I have more than seen her! I had to call an ambulance earlier on. She went into labour.'

'What do you mean?' Sophie asked, unable to take in what she was being told. 'Gabi's not pregnant…' But even as Sophie said it, Gabi's avoidance of her in the last few months and the new distance between them was starting to make sense.

'She's more than six months gone,' Anya said. 'I had no idea either until her waters broke. I think the baby will come tonight.'

'Is there anyone with her?' Sophie asked, while knowing that there was nothing she could really do.

'I think she was going to call her mother once she got to the hospital.'

It was a rather distracted Sophie that went in for the evening briefing. Here she would be told where she would be working tonight, though it didn't really matter to Sophie. She just wanted to know what was going on with her friend.

'Are you listening, Sophie?' Benita checked.

'Of course,' Sophie said, and forced herself to at least look as if she was paying attention.

'Could you help with the set-up of the ballroom for the wedding tomorrow? Things have fallen rather behind.'

Sophie nodded and wrote the instructions down in

her notebook as Benita spoke on to the rest of the gathered staff.

'Sultan Alim has had to fly home unexpectedly,' Benita continued, 'which makes things a little easier on this busy night. Laura, you and I shall service his floor when there is a moment to breathe. Now, in Presidential Suite B we have Signor Conti...'

Sophie felt her heart soar and her cheeks warm at the sound of his name.

'He's an important guest at the Grande Lucia,' Benita carried on. 'Today he has declined to have the suite serviced. However, should he change his mind, Inga and Laura, could you see to it promptly, please?' Benita's voice was sharp and sometimes Sophie was rather sure that Benita knew what Inga got up to. 'Please remember that Signor Conti is a serious contender to purchase this hotel. He may well be your boss in the future, so please be on your best behaviour. Remember that he is here to observe the staff and glean as much information as he can about the running of the hotel.'

Sophie felt as if the floor had shifted beneath her. The handover continued but Sophie heard not a word. She wanted to call out, to ask Benita to explain further about Bastiano. Still drenched in horror, she could not quite take in what had just been said, but Benita was wrapping things up and gave her team a smile. 'Let's get to work, then.'

It was a shaken and tearful Sophie who did her best to work through the night.

Gabi's boss, Bernadetta, had been called in to accomplish overnight all the work to be done. She was a poisonous woman at the best of times, and on this night she worked the fragile Sophie hard.

The ribbons she had her tie over and over, the chairs

she had her lug and move, and she screeched at Sophie to concentrate as for the umpteenth time she had to lay the place cards according to the table plan.

Finally, *finally*, around two in the morning, Benita popped her head in the ballroom and told Sophie it was time for her break.

'Is everything okay?' Ronaldo, the doorman, asked as Sophie stepped outside the kitchens for a breath of air. Ronaldo was also on his break and having a cigarette.

'I'll be glad when it is morning,' Sophie admitted. 'It is awful working with Bernadetta and there is all this talk of the hotel being taken over.'

'I know! Let's hope it's Di Savo,' Ronaldo said. 'He has a hotel here in Rome.'

'What about the other one?' Sophie fished.

'Conti?' Ronaldo said, and raised his eyebrows. 'He's a risk taker, a loose cannon.'

'In what way?'

'In every way. He and Di Savo are sworn enemies. Security was told to be on high alert, what with the two of them staying here at the same time.'

'Really?'

Ronaldo nodded. 'Especially because last night Di Savo was entertaining Conti's guest.' He gave a knowing eye raise. 'We just have to hope that Di Savo wins the bid as well as the girl. Bastiano Conti's a cold-hearted bastard—that much I know.'

'How do you know?'

'I'm the doorman,' Ronaldo said. 'He often stays here as he and the sultan are friends. Believe me when I say I see all that goes on. I wouldn't let my sister within a mile radius of him.'

'They're friends?' Sophie checked, recalling Bastiano's skilled questioning—he had acted as if he was surprised that Alim was a sultan.

'Good friends.' Ronaldo nodded. 'Though I thought the sultan had better taste.'

It was bad enough that she had slept with the potential new boss, but it was utterly humiliating the way she had been taken in by him. Bastiano had had her opening up and speaking to him as if they were lovers.

That was what she had thought they were.

What had taken place had for Sophie been so wonderful, but now it was tainted.

She had thought he'd been asking all those questions to find out about her, but instead he had been playing her all along.

Thank goodness she hadn't told him that she thought Inga was up to tricks. Sophie did not like her, but neither did she want to get her into trouble—it was a dismissible offence.

And one that she herself had committed.

Oh, whatever way she looked at it, she was in trouble.

Her job was the biggest and proudest achievement of her life. Sophie loved coming to work each day, she loved her colleagues and the friends she had made.

And at any moment now it might all be taken away.

By morning, the ballroom was somehow ready for the upcoming wedding but Sophie was no less frantic. When Benita asked if someone could go and help out with the breakfast service, Sophie did not put up her hand.

She simply did not know how to face him.

Bastiano was more than ready to face Sophie, though.

He had woken at around midnight having had the best sleep he had known in a very long time.

It had taken a moment to register that she had gone. Bastiano had even gone to the bathroom, half hoping to find her lying up to her neck in bubbles as he had earlier in the day.

Recalling what Sophie had said about liking order, he had called the butler and asked that he send someone to service the room.

To his disappointment it was Inga, the woman who had brought the *gelato*, who'd arrived, along with another chambermaid.

'You were working this afternoon,' Bastiano commented.

'They asked me to do a split shift.' Inga smiled.

He placed his breakfast order.

Shakshuka for Sophie and Sicilian pastries for him, only this time he asked for summer berries and a bottle of champagne to be served with the juice.

Finally morning arrived and there was a knock at the door; he heard the trolley being wheeled in and then another soft knock on his bedroom door.

'Entra,' Bastiano said.

He had been in the industry long enough to know Sophie would have no say where she was assigned, yet as he sat up to a soft *'Buongiorno...'* he lay back down when he realised that it was not Sophie.

The curtains were opened and the shutters too, but Bastiano deliberately closed his eyes.

'Can I serve you breakfast?' Inga asked, when protocol dictated she should leave rather than speak.

'No.'

'Is there anything else I can do for you, Signor Conti?'

He opened his eyes and though imperceptible to many, Bastiano knew the ropes well and could both hear and see the veiled offer; yes, Inga would love to be in bed with the boss.

'You can leave.' His voice was curt and with a flick of his wrist he dismissed her.

Inga left and the minutes dragged by ever more slowly as Sophie failed to appear.

It edged close to seven and still Sophie did not arrive. Bastiano knew only too well how bad it would look if he were to call down to the front desk and ask after her.

There was nothing he could do except wait.

And, when the morning was already misbehaving, Bastiano got up and poured his own coffee, but by then it was far too cool. He flicked open the newspaper and suddenly his day got a whole lot worse.

There was an image of Raul Di Savo, his nemesis, sitting in a café, one Bastiano recognised as being opposite the hotel. And he was holding hands with Lydia Hayward.

So she hadn't been catching up with friends after all.

Bastiano and Raul both had colourful reputations and both knew how the other worked.

Raul must have found out that Lydia was a guest of his, Bastiano surmised. Hostilities had just increased tenfold, and he screwed up the paper and tossed it to the floor.

His phone rang. It was Maurice, spluttering his apologies that Lydia remained unavailable and asking when they might meet to speak about the castle.

But Bastiano had no interest in Maurice's draughty old building now.

'We shan't be meeting, Maurice. And when you see your stepdaughter, tell her that the reason for Raul Di Savo's interest in her is simply to get back at me. There is no more to it than that.'

He was in no doubt that Maurice would indeed pass

the message on and, he hoped, at the very least, that it would cause Raul and Lydia to have a major row.

Next he called down to the front desk and asked that his bags be packed and his transport arranged.

Forget Rome! Forget fragrant baths and spiced Sicilian pastries! And most of all, forget Sophie!

Bastiano was back to being a bastard.

CHAPTER SIX

SOPHIE HAD SIMPLY not known how to face Bastiano.

It wasn't just that she was frightened for her job, Sophie felt angry and humiliated—sure that he had been silently laughing at her all along.

And so, after the longest night at work, instead of heading to his suite she headed for home. Once there, she called the hospital to find out what she could about Gabi but they gave out little information.

'Can I visit?' she asked. After learning the hours when she could see Gabi, she decided that she would go in the evening, before the start of her next shift.

She felt sick at the thought of walking into work and positive that she was going to be in deep trouble.

Perhaps he wouldn't buy the hotel, Sophie thought as she tried to sleep. Though there was little solace that that would contain things, for she now knew that Bastiano was a personal friend of Sultan Alim.

And as nice as Alim was, he had a fierce reputation with women too.

Sophie lay there with visions of Bastiano thanking Alim for the *nice surprise* sent to his suite.

And yet for all her worries there remained the absence of regret.

Today, Sophie knew, could so easily have been her first wedding anniversary.

And so that evening, as she walked onto the maternity ward to visit her friend, she knew full well that it could easily have been her sitting pale in the bed, having just given birth, with Luigi by her side.

No.

She might have to suffer the consequences work-wise, but her first time would always be as she had wanted it to be.

Even if she lost her job.

'Sophie...' Gabi started to cry as soon as Sophie walked in.

She had bought her a bunch of flowers and a little lemon-coloured bear for the baby, who was nowhere in sight.

'It's okay,' Sophie said, taking her friend in her arms and not really knowing what to say. 'Is the baby okay? The nurses wouldn't tell me anything.'

'I had a little girl,' Gabi said. 'Lucia.'

'And how is she doing?'

'She's in the nursery. She's very early but they say that for her size she is really well.'

'I bought this for her.'

Sophie handed over the little bear and Gabi smiled when she saw her baby's first toy.

'I can't believe she's here,' Gabi said.

'Believe me...' Sophie's eyes widened '...neither can anyone! All the staff are in shock. Why on earth didn't you tell me that you were pregnant?'

'It seemed wrong to be telling everyone when I haven't even told her father...' Gabi admitted.

Sophie waited, but Gabi shook her head; clearly she still wasn't ready to reveal who the father was.

It didn't stop Sophie from trying to work it out, though!

'Ronaldo?' Sophie asked, because she often saw them chatting.

'Oh, please,' Gabi said, and then through her tears she started to laugh. 'Ronaldo?'

'Well, he is good looking.' Sophie shrugged. 'And you two are friendly.'

'I talk to Ronaldo because he knows all the gossip,' Gabi said.

Not *all* the gossip, Sophie hoped.

She stayed for a little while and promised to come in and visit again, but all too soon she was heading to work, terrified of what awaited her yet conflicted, for she knew she secretly hoped to see Bastiano again.

Benita gave her a smile when a blushing Sophie joined the group for the briefing.

'The wedding is in full swing,' Benita said, and took them through the plans for the night ahead. 'Signor Conti checked out early this morning.'

Nobody heard as Sophie's heart dropped.

She stood, staring at her pencil poised over her notepad, and there were tears in her eyes as Benita spoke on.

'The staff have been busy all day and have not been able to service the presidential suite. Sophie, could you make a start, please, and I'll come and help you as soon as I can, then you can go and help with the clear up once the wedding guests have left.'

The workload was so heavy that Benita suggested she didn't stay for the rest of handover and so, with a heavy heart, Sophie made her way up in the elevator, the same one in which she had once floated back down to earth.

Each presidential suite had its own butler's pantry and its own cleaning supply room so there was no trolley to collect. She let herself in and saw that it was a lot neater than when she had left it.

Sophie walked through the vacant lounge to the master bedroom. On a silver trolley stood an untouched breakfast. She lifted the domes and saw the pastries and *shakshuka*, but there were summer berries too. What brought tears to her eyes, though, was that there was an unopened bottle of champagne standing in a bucket of water, and she knew he had ordered it for her.

It was the most romantic thing that had ever happened to her.

Or, rather, that had never happened.

Maybe she had been too hasty, Sophie thought.

There was the expensive scent of him in the air and the memory of them in her mind.

Sophie was quite sure she was going to be fired anyway and so, just for a moment, she lay on the bed where he had slept and tried to tell her heart to slow down.

Please, let her job be safe!

Which meant she had better get on and do it, for Benita might well be here soon and so she peeled herself from the bed.

First she wheeled out the breakfast trolley and did a little pick up of rubbish. There was a screwed-up newspaper on the floor and when she smoothed it out there was a photo of Raul Di Savo and a pale blonde beauty, sitting together in the café opposite the hotel.

It was Lydia, Sophie was sure.

This must have been the reason that Bastiano had checked out early.

His rapid departure had nothing to do with her—Sophie knew she didn't wasn't so much as a pawn in his games.

She had been nothing more than a diversion—that was all.

Sophie scrubbed the bath where they had lain smiling and chatting; it hurt to recall him joining her and then carrying her through to the bed that she now stripped back and remade.

To service a presidential suite to standard took ages. Benita had said that she would come and help but, of course, she was too busy and so it was Sophie who had to make sure that it was done to perfection.

And it hurt.

It was some considerable time later that Benita arrived with her check list and together they went through the suite.

Ornaments, decanters, glasses, furniture, all had to be gleaming. Every feature down to the last detail was checked and ticked off.

Two pairs of eyes were needed as generally, though inadvertently, something was missed.

Not on this night.

She had erased every last detail of them.

'All ready for the next guest.' Benita smiled. 'Very well done, Sophie—Signor Conti always leaves a storm behind him.'

'Really?' Sophie couldn't help but fish for details.

'He likes the women and knows how to party.' Benita gave a tight smile. 'You have done an excellent job,' she said as she flicked off the lights. 'You would never know that anyone had been here.'

Now Sophie just had to tell her heart the same.

CHAPTER SEVEN

REALLY, HER BIRTHDAY was just another day.

Sophie got up late and had coffee with her flatmate, Teresa, who then headed off to her waitressing job.

It had been Teresa's birthday last month and Sophie had stopped on the way home from work and bought a cake.

It shouldn't hurt that Teresa made no mention of the date.

She made too much of things, Sophie told herself. She pulled on a top and skirt and left a little earlier than usual for her twilight shift at the Grande Lucia.

She unlocked the mailbox in the foyer of her building and there was a small wad of mail; Sophie found that she was holding her breath as she flicked through it.

Nothing.

There had been no phone call this morning from her parents and now not even a card.

Her oldest brother had called the other week and told her that Luigi still came for dinner each week, only now he hit the wine.

'Do you think that makes me want to come home and marry him?' Sophie had said and ended the call.

They didn't get it.

Bastiano had.

Even after all these months just the thought of him could stop Sophie in the street.

Just the memory of that day was enough to make her smile—a little gift she could open and treasure on a day when she felt forgotten and small.

There was still a little while before her shift commenced and Sophie decided that she would drop in on Gabi and see how she and little Lucia were doing. It had been a while since they had caught up. Gabi had only been back at work for a couple of weeks and had already been on an international trip to help organise Sultan Alim's upcoming wedding while her mother cared for Lucia.

It all sounded terribly glamorous to Sophie.

'Sophie!' Gabi gave her a tired smile as she opened the door. 'It's good to see you!'

Little Lucia was crying and Sophie was more than happy to hold her as Gabi made them a quick lunch. 'What time is your shift?' Gabi asked.

'I start at two,' Sophie said. 'How was your trip overseas?'

'It was…' Gabi gave a tight shrug. 'It was hard leaving Lucia.'

'But what was it like?' Sophie asked. She had never been out of Italy, let alone flown to the Middle East! But then she remembered that Gabi had had a bit of a crush on Alim and guessed her questions might be insensitive. 'How was Alim?'

'I didn't really see him.'

'So you don't know who's buying the hotel?'

Gabi shook her head.

'Everyone is worried for their jobs,' Sophie sighed.

'It should be okay,' Gabi tried to reassure her. 'Raul

Di Savo has many hotels, one of them is here in Rome. I am sure there wouldn't be too many changes.'

'What about if the other one gets it?'

'God help us all then,' Gabi sighed. 'Conti takes over old buildings, guts them and then modernises them...' She pulled a face. 'Sultan Alim has spent the past two years restoring the hotel. Conti will ruin all that...'

'He might not,' Sophie countered, though she recalled him talking about Lydia and the castle that she lived in and how much work it would have been.

Was it all just business for him?

'Apparently, he turns all his acquisitions into upmarket rehab facilities,' Gabi said. 'I can't imagine there would be many weddings being held at the Grande Lucia if that is the case.' Then she gave a tight shrug. 'Not that it will matter much to me. I am not sure I can hold on to this job.' Gabi explained things a little better. 'My mother wants me to get a job with more regular hours.'

'Is she still cross about the baby?'

Gabi nodded. 'She has started to come around—at least we're finally speaking. In truth, I wouldn't be able to work without her support.'

'What about Lucia's father?' Sophie asked.

'I'm not ready to talk about him,' Gabi admitted.

'Fair enough,' Sophie said, and glanced at the time. 'I'd better go. I'll come and see you both soon.'

'Make sure that you do.'

And so her birthday went unnoticed again, and of course Sophie didn't blame her friend. Gabi had enough on her mind as it was.

Sophie walked the back streets, down the alley and entered the hotel via the side entrance, then walked through the kitchen and to the locker area.

There was a pile of clean uniforms with her name

on that were freshly starched and uncomfortably tight and scratchy when she put one on; quickly, she re-did her hair.

The hotel was very full, they were told at the briefing. There was a high turnover of rooms to make up and no time to waste if they were to get everything done.

Benita gave out assignments for the day. 'Sophie, you are on the twelfth floor, odd numbers.'

Sophie nodded. The twelfth floor housed the cheaper rooms, all without any landmark views and were just plain hard work.

'Oh, and, Sophie,' Benita added, and Sophie waited to be told that when she had finished she was to go and help out Inga, who always seemed to be running behind, but instead there was some surprising news. 'You have a delivery to pick up at Reception.'

'A delivery?'

'Yes. Is it your birthday or something?'

Sophie nodded and her heart started to beat fast, wondering if maybe, just maybe, her parents had sent her something here.

She was almost bouncing on the spot for the briefing to finish and when it did, instead of heading straight up to the twelfth floor, she went straight to the reception desk.

'There is a delivery for me?' Sophie said to Anya.

'Indeed there is,' Anya said. 'Lucky girl.'

Even as she came out of the cloakroom, Sophie knew that the flowers Anya held were not from her parents, for this was not the type of gift they would ever give.

It wasn't a big bouquet; in fact, it was a small posy that Anya handed to her, wrapped in cream tissue paper and exuding understated elegance.

The flowers really were exquisite.

Perhaps a hundred miniature roses in the softest

creams, all edged in the palest green. Each one looked as if it had been individually painted with the most skilled brush, and the scent when she drew the bouquet close to her face was like inhaling summer.

'It's stunning,' Anya sighed. 'All the staff have been coming in and out for a peek.'

And as if to prove her point, Inga came over.

'They're nice,' she said.

'I think Sophie has an admirer,' Anya teased. 'Come on, open the card.'

'Who are they from?' Inga asked, but when Sophie opened the card it was blank.

'I don't know,' she lied.

Or was it the truth?

For the Bastiano Conti everyone spoke of did not send flowers and was guaranteed to forget.

Had he remembered?

Or was this an elaborate gift from Gabi?

Even an expensive gift from a stressed, broke, new mum made rather more sense than it coming from Bastiano, yet her heart knew they were from him, and each bloom felt like a tiny kiss to her soul.

'They need to go in water,' Anya told her. 'I can do that for you and you can collect them when you go home.'

'Thank you,' Sophie said, but she was reluctant to let them go and so she selected one and coiled it into her messy bun.

Oh, the twelfth floor had never seen such a smiling maid, for even if the roses weren't from Bastiano, it was simply nice to know that someone had remembered.

And yet the flutter in her heart told her that that someone was him.

'Benita's looking for you,' Laura told her. 'She wants to see you now in the staffroom.'

There was still that slight edge of dread, Sophie thought as she took the elevator down. Still that fear that she was about to be found out.

But it had been months ago, she consoled herself.

Three months, in fact.

And, Sophie knew, Bastiano had stayed a couple of times at the Grande Lucia since then, though never when she had been working. Sadly, she wasn't privy to the guest list and tended to find out about these things after the event.

But surely, Sophie thought, if word was going to get out then it would have happened by now.

Her palms were just a little slippery as she opened the door to the staffroom.

'Buon Compleanno!'

'Happy birthday' was being called out to her and there was even a cake with candles and jugs of soft drink.

'Your favourite chef made this for you,' Benita told her. 'He says next year a little more notice would be nice. You should have told us!'

The chef had made her *torta setteveli*, or seven veils cake. Layers of chocolate mousse, hazelnut, praline, cream and sponge, all topped with a chocolate glaze.

It was the last thing that Sophie had expected. To have her colleagues gather and wish her a happy birthday meant everything and she thanked her lucky stars for the day she had been given a job at the Grande Lucia.

The cake tasted like chocolate silk and was a mouthwatering slice of home.

'Actually,' Sophie admitted, 'this tastes better than any I have ever had.'

'Well, don't have too much,' Benita teased, and gave a little pinch to her waist as Sophie went for a second slice. 'Or you will be asking for new uniforms.'

Sophie laughed; the cake was decadent and rich indeed but that would not stop her from having a second slice. Soon, the staff who had gathered drifted back to their responsibilities and the remains were left in the fridge for Sophie to take back to her flat.

She sailed through the rest of her shift. The flowers and cake had lifted her, yet home would have to wait for as her shift neared its end she was offered an hour of overtime.

'Sophie,' Benita called her, 'we have an important guest arriving. Are you able to stay back?'

'Of course.'

Overtime was always welcome, and it was also nice to be asked.

They raced up to the presidential suite—though cleaned, it had not had the finishing touches for an important guest.

It was always hard to be up here, but Sophie did her best not to show it, to carry on as if it was just another room that she was preparing, rather than the site of her magical day with Bastiano.

'Why don't these stars give a little more notice?' Sophie asked as the champagne and flowers were brought in and she and Benita turned back the vast bed.

'Because they don't have to; they know we will always jump to their tune,' Benita said as she turned down the silk sheets. 'Anyway,' she added, 'it's not some famous rock star coming to the Grande Lucia tonight, it is Signor Conti, the soon-to-be...' She paused, because the news had not yet been confirmed.

And Sophie just scrunched the sheet in her hand as, unwittingly, Benita let her know that not only was Bastiano due to arrive tonight but that soon he would be taking over the hotel.

'I should not have said that,' Benita admitted.

'It's fine,' Sophie answered. 'It shan't go any further.'

'Make sure it doesn't. The contracts have not yet been signed and Alim wants to leave any formal announcement until they are.' Benita let out a long sigh, but now that Sophie knew, Benita admitted to a little of what was on her mind. 'Really, I wish it had been the other. Conti is bad news.'

'Bad news?' Sophie said, and while she usually acquiesced to Benita, suddenly she saw red. She was sick of hearing everyone bad-mouth Bastiano.

'I doubt he got to be a billionaire by accident,' Sophie said tartly to her senior. 'I think the Grande Lucia would be very lucky to have someone as astute as Signor Conti as its new owner.'

Benita raised an eyebrow as Sophie sprang to his defence but decided against saying anything further about her potential new boss!

'The room looks perfect,' Sophie said, blushing a little at having spoken her mind to her senior.

She put a slip of paper by the bed, informing him about the weather tomorrow—she wanted to add a heart.

Benita went to close the shutters and drapes so that all the esteemed guest had to do was peel off his clothes and drop into the sumptuous bed.

It seemed a shame to block out the view but that was how things were done during turndown.

The lights were dimmed and the room ticked off on the service sheet, and then Benita did one more sweep of the drawing room and lounge before exiting to the corridor.

And Sophie stood there, her heart hammering, uncertain what she should do.

Oh, she wanted so badly to speak to him—she simply had to find out if she was about to be in trouble, but more than that she needed to see him again.

And then Sophie knew how to let Bastiano know that she was thinking of him.

She walked over to the drapes and opened them, pushing back the shutters, and remembered that moment when her heart had found him.

It truly felt as if it had.

Not the man everyone spoke of so ominously, more the man who had smiled and made her melt.

She looked out on Rome at night and recalled turning to his smile.

'What were you doing?' Benita asked when Sophie joined Benita in the corridor.

'I was just checking that I had written the weather down for tomorrow. Everything is looking perfect.'

'Then you can go home now, Sophie. When are you back on?'

'In the morning, at six.'

'Well, go and get some sleep.'

Sophie walked slowly down the corridor and, instead of taking the elevator to the basement, she went to the foyer, hoping for what, she did not know.

A glimpse of Bastiano perhaps?

But he had not arrived.

Benita had already told her that she would be on house duties tomorrow and working in the foyer. Certainly she would not be up in the presidential suites.

Sophie knew she had to speak with him.

But how?

Her voice might be recognised, or perhaps he would not take the call.

As Sophie reached Reception she thought about hanging around to wait for his arrival.

'Sophie?' Inga stopped as she walked past. 'What are you hanging around for?'

'I had some overtime,' Sophie said, 'but I think I dropped my notebook…'

And in that moment she made up her mind and turned for the elevators.

It was wrong; she could well be fired for what she was about to do, and Sophie's heart was hammering as she pressed the buttons that would take her to the floor from which she had just come.

She had to use her staff pass as the presidential suites had limited access.

He might bring a woman back with him, or a friend, Sophie suddenly thought in panic. The butler would be there, and also there would be the bellboys delivering his luggage. There were a million things that could go wrong, but she simply had to speak to him, to thank him for the beautiful roses.

If Bastiano was to be the new owner, then she was probably about to lose her job anyway, so she let herself into the suite.

The lights were dimmed and there was soft music playing to welcome him.

She touched nothing.

Sophie sat on a chair by a writing bureau and waited as the moments ticked by, but then finally there were voices.

Voices!

She stood from the chair and went into a small alcove where the staff would be unlikely to venture.

Sophie stood in the dark, her heart hammering, realising the foolishness of her actions and anticipating his anger…yet there was also excitement curling in her stomach for finally she would see him again.

'I have no luggage...' She heard his deep voice tell the butler that there was nothing to unpack, and then a terse, 'I can pour my own drink!'

Bastiano simply wanted the man gone.

The butler closed the door and finally there was silence.

What the hell was he doing here?

What was he doing, putting in an offer for a hotel he didn't even want, just to score a point over Raul?

Raul didn't want it either.

He had paid Bastiano a visit the other day. At first Bastiano had assumed he had come to argue over the hotel.

Instead Raul had asked for Lydia's address.

Bastiano's price?

The return of his mother's ring.

This morning, just as he had finished speaking with the florist to arrange Sophie's birthday surprise, a packaged had arrived.

Bastiano hadn't yet opened it.

Now, all these years on, he gazed at the ring, remembering Maria trying it on and holding it up to the light.

Yet memory was not kind.

Now that he held the ring in his hand, long-buried memories were starting to come back.

'Give me back the ring, Maria.'

He could hear his younger voice attempting to hold on to his temper as she had claimed his mother's ring as her own.

A couple of hours later, still wearing it, she had died.

He placed it on the gleaming table, for holding it kicked up black dusty memories that were best left undisturbed.

Bastiano stood and poured a cognac. Looking around the suite, he remembered the last time he had been here, reading the paper, finding out about Raul and Lydia, but then he remembered the hours before that, the bliss of a day away from the world, and so clear were the memories that for a moment he was sure he could recall the scent of Sophie.

He could.

Bastiano opened his eyes and wondered if it was Sophie who had prepared the room; as he filled out the breakfast order, he wondered if she might be the one to serve it.

He hoped so.

And then he heard a movement.

Her intention had been to call out, to step out, but now she stood in the dark, terrified by the predicament that she had placed herself in.

'Sophie?'

She heard her name, he knew she was here and she knew she had to reveal herself.

'I didn't know how else to see you...' she started as she stepped from the shadows and walked towards him.

Her presence was enough for Bastiano to know that this was the real reason he was here in Rome. Sophie was the reason the contracts were unsigned, and that he'd had his lawyers stringing things along, for while he did, there was a chance to see her again.

'If you had wanted to see me then you should have come back that morning,' Bastiano said.

'I was scared I was about to lose my job!' She could hear that her voice was raised. There was fear mixed in with desire for, yes, the months that had passed had dimmed her recall of his absolute power. 'You never told me you were thinking of buying the place. Why did you lie?'

'I never lied.'

'You did.' Sophie raised an accusing finger. 'I would have never told you the things that I did—'

'And I knew that,' Bastiano hotly responded. 'I wanted to keep us the same.'

'We're not the same.' She came right up to his face, and all the hurt and anger she had held in these months flooded out. 'You're the rich man and I'm the maid, how could we ever be the same...?'

'You know that we are.' He too was nearly shouting. 'In here we are.'

Weeks and months of denial and anger met now and she loathed his absolute beauty, that, even now, had absolute power over her. And in turn he loathed the chink in his armour that bore her name, because he could not forget and he could not move on.

He kissed her hard and she fought with herself not to kiss him back.

'What happens when you own it?' she asked. 'My job is everything to me...'

'I'm not buying the hotel.' He stole more kisses and when she pulled back her mouth he simply found it again.

'So why are you here?'

For this.

He didn't say it, but now his mouth did.

Today had been hell and he craved oblivion. Their teeth clashed as their mouths met once again, and his tongue tethered her fury as she returned his fierce kiss.

Bastiano went for her uniform and she heard the rip of the buttons and she was kissing him back and crying as she tasted him again.

'Now we are the same,' he told her as very deliberately he removed her uniform, pushing it down her arms and then past her hips so it fell to the floor.

'No.'

For he was still the rich man in his expensive suit and she stood in drab underwear, but soon he was removing that too.

He turned her and kissed her so that her back was to the wall and his suited body pressed against her naked flesh.

Sophie closed her eyes and drank in his scent, recalling her silent desire to know this man less restrained. And now she knew, for the sound of his zipper and his ragged breath in her ear turned rage to desire, and it was she who held his head now, kissing him back hard as he wrapped her leg around his waist.

'Never let me down,' she begged, and her words were nonsensical for even as he drove into her, even as he consumed her, Sophie knew she was opening herself to hurt, and that tomorrow the countdown would resume and abstinence must surely start over again.

He placed one hand on the wall behind her while the other dug into the cheek of her buttock. He was as coarse in delivery as her violent need required. She did not understand how the woman who had trembled and hidden only a matter of moments ago now coiled naked around him.

Now they were the same.

Matched in desire and lost in lust.

'I thought of you…' he told her, and whether or not she believed him those words tipped her.

He felt the shift and lifted her other leg, so she was wrapped firmly around his hips and their kisses were intense as he spilled deep inside.

'You're going to get me fired,' Sophie whispered as their bodies began to relax and now, slowly, he let her down.

'Never,' Bastiano said. 'Are you supposed to be working now?'

'Not until morning.'

'Good,' he told her. 'Then we have all night.'

CHAPTER EIGHT

'YOU PREPARED MY SUITE,' Bastiano said as they stepped into the master bedroom and he saw the gorgeous night view of Rome.

'I did.'

Sophie did not feel disadvantaged at being the one who was undressed, for indeed she got to slip straight into bed and to lie watching as Bastiano got undressed.

'I wanted you to remember me when you came in.'

'I don't need a view to remember you.' It was undoubtedly the most romantic thing he had ever said but she appeared not to notice its significance. In fact, Sophie thought she was being fed a line and lay there sulking as he went and had a quick shower.

'You got my flowers.' He could see the tiny rose that was now knotted in her hair but as beautiful as her flowers had been, Sophie was not going to let him off that easily.

'Three months late.'

'You were the one who didn't come back,' Bastiano pointed out, taking his time to dry himself.

'And you were the one who failed to tell me you were thinking of buying the place. Can you imagine how it felt to find out?'

'I meant to tell you before you left for work,' he admitted.

'I was scared for my job and I kept thinking of all the things I'd told you.'

'Sophie, I was hardly sitting taking notes.' He got into bed and the soapy clean scent of him was divine. 'I wasn't even thinking about the hotel, I was just…' And it was he who was quiet then because now he allowed himself to look back properly at that perfect day.

'I thought you were staying for another night,' she said. 'You were booked in until the Monday.'

'I left angry,' he admitted. 'I found out…' Bastiano shook his head, not wanting to bring up the feud with Raul.

He was tired of it.

But Sophie had long since guessed the reason he had walked.

'You found out about Raul and Lydia?'

He looked over and gave her a slow smile. 'Nothing gets past you.'

'With the right education, I'd have ruled the world.' Sophie smiled and then told him how she knew. 'I saw their picture in a screwed-up newspaper, I guessed you had seen it.'

'I had.'

They lay together and he pulled her close so that she lay in the crook of his arm, and it was such a nice place to be.

'He came to see me the other day. We hadn't spoken for fifteen years. I thought it was to argue over the hotel but he wanted to find out where Lydia lived.'

'Did you tell him?'

'For a price,' Bastiano said, and thought of the ring.

'Why do you two hate each other so?'

'We always have,' Bastiano told her. 'Our families have always been rivals.'

It was the easy version of the story.

It was too complex a conversation for ships that passed in the night, yet they lay there and stared out at the view, Sophie nestled in the crook of his arm. This was more than a casual encounter, Bastiano knew.

Sophie had arrived with no warning.

She had stepped onto the stage of his life, but there was so much debris, so much damage, and he did not know how to clear it. He told her a little of the complicated version.

'We used to be friends,' he admitted. 'When we were growing up our families frowned on it but we didn't care, and as teenagers we thought we could take on the world. Then Raul left for university.'

'What did you do?'

'I worked in my uncle's bar.' There was no point prettying it up—he and Raul had been enemies for a reason. 'After he left I slept with his mother.' He awaited her recoil or the uplift of her head and narrowing eyes but she just lay there. 'We had an affair, and when it was exposed she died in a car crash.'

'How old were you?' Sophie asked.

'Seventeen. I wasn't exactly innocent before that, though. In the end I tried to persuade her to leave her husband and come away with me but she refused. Raul believes I as good as killed her.'

'Were you the one driving?'

He frowned at Sophie's question.

'No.'

'Well, then, how could it be your fault?'

Sophie lifted herself up on her arm and he glimpsed again her absolute refusal to simply acquiesce.

'Her husband had found out about us.'

'How old was she?'

'Thirty-four,' Bastiano said. He had thought Maria closer to her forties at the time but really she had not been much older than he was now.

Sophie's lip curled. *'Poutana.'*

'Hey!' He rose to Maria's defence, as he always had. 'We were in…' Bastiano halted but a little too late, for Sophie knew what he had been about to say.

'In love?' she sneered, and then shook her head. 'That's not love.'

'How would you know?' he demanded.

'I know what love isn't,' Sophie responded hotly. 'I left home because, for all my lack of experience in the matter, I believed that love should make you smile.'

'Perhaps—if you live on the cover of a chocolate box.'

'So, if it was love, why didn't she leave her husband?'

'She was very religious,' Bastiano said. 'When Maria was growing up she wanted to be a nun.'

Sophie gave a derisive snort. 'Why wasn't she one, then?'

'Because at sixteen she got pregnant with Raul.'

Bastiano reached over and turned out the light but, far from annoyed at her scathing assessment of Maria, he was actually touched that somehow, on rather black evidence, she was defending him.

They lay in silence but far from sleep.

It was difficult to speak of that time but it was also hard to hear.

'It was Raul you fought with?' she asked.

'After the funeral.' Bastiano nodded. 'That was the easy part—the next day we found out she had left money in her will to be divided between him and me. He thinks I knew that she had money…'

'Did you?'

'No,' Bastiano said. 'Raul told me he'd watch me go under, he said I was nothing without her money.'

'So she left you enough to buy the Grande Lucia?'

'No.' He gave a low laugh at the thought. 'I bought a derelict building...' He thought of how the Old Convent had been then. 'There were no roads to access it. There weren't many tourists then in the west and I bought it for a song. I've bought a few more since then.'

'You could have blown that money,' Sophie said. 'Instead, look at all you have done.'

She did not know the scope of his wealth, just that he could consider the purchase of this hotel, which told her how much Bastiano had done with the start he felt he had not deserved.

In Sophie's mind he had earned every cent.

'Last month,' Sophie said into the darkness, 'when I called home, my brother told me that Luigi had taken to drink.'

Bastiano said nothing.

'It's my fault apparently.' She turned and saw his strong profile and that his eyes were open but he did not look at her. 'As I said to my brother, I'm quite sure there was a problem long before he had me to blame it on.'

'You certainly take no prisoners.' He looked at her then and she heard rather than saw his smile. 'Were you always tough?'

'I had to learn to be,' Sophie told him, 'and fast. I have five brothers and all of them would be perfectly happy to have me pick up after them. I pick up after myself, unless, of course, I am being paid.'

Bastiano slept, but Sophie lay there awake, troubled by her own words on the subject of love.

He made her smile.

Oh, not in a chocolate box way.

Just the thought of him, and the memory of them, had elicited more smiles in the last three months than she had collected in a lifetime before that.

And the world turned too fast when they were in bed, for when she reached for water, Sophie could make out the outline of the Colosseum when before it had been wrapped in darkness.

As she lay back down he pulled her in so that her head lay on his chest and she watched the sky, willing morning not to come.

His hand was on her arm and she toyed idly with the snake of black hair that had entranced her when she had gone to reach for the plate that first morning.

There was no reason now not to move the sheet, no reason left to be shy, and so she slipped her hand lower, feeling him grow hard under her fingers.

Her face felt warm on his chest and his hand was still on her shoulder as she slid down.

She had no real idea what she was doing, but he rose to her palm as if to greet her. She felt the warmth nudge her cheek and as she kissed just the tip and then knelt and ran her tongue down the side, he grew to the length of her face. This she knew, for she worked her tongue up and down, absorbed in the task at hand.

Bastiano moved the hair from her eyes.

And then as she ventured deep he took her hair and coiled it around his hand, just so that he could see her.

Usually he preferred a curtain of hair, but with Sophie he liked watching the stretch of her jaw and then the tease of her tongue.

He liked watching while she closed her eyes and they were lost to each other, utterly oblivious to a world waking up outside.

So oblivious that the sound of the main door opening went unheard.

Bastiano moaning her name did not.

'Sophie…'

One hand was stroking her bottom, the other wrapped in her hair, and she was lost in the moment as he came to her mouth.

And Inga stood there, jealousy rising like bile as she saw Sophie's uniform a puddle on the floor.

Sophie, always sweet and smiling, and yet so judgmental of Inga, was at it too.

And with their soon-to-be boss—Bastiano Conti.

Oh, the two of them were not quite finished yet and remained oblivious to her arrival in the suite, but Inga's eyes lit on a ring, and she knew exactly how she would punish Sophie for her hypocrisy.

She slipped the ring into the pocket of Sophie's discarded uniform and quietly wheeled the trolley back out, then she took out a pen and changed his breakfast order to seven.

'Hey.' Inga wheeled the trolley back to the kitchen and spoke with the chef. 'Signor Conti's breakfast is not due for another hour. Luckily I noticed.'

Very lucky.

For some.

Explain that, Sophie!

CHAPTER NINE

'I'M GOING TO be late,' Sophie warned as they showered together.

'Don't go to work today.'

'You might have some sway if you were the new boss...' She laughed. 'No, I am going in so I can be guilt-free on my days off.'

'How long are you off for?'

'Two days and two nights.'

She quickly dressed and, yes, she was going to work but with conditions attached.

'This time you're to come back,' he warned, taking her in his arms. 'Tonight we'll go out, somewhere nice.'

And she frowned because, yes, it was an age-old problem but Sophie truly had nothing suitable for a date with Bastiano Conti. Luckily, he read her concern.

'I'll take care of everything.'

As she left, Bastiano was ready to plan their evening.

More than that, he was considering flying her home.

Never had he had any inclination to bring anyone back to the Old Convent, but telling her his history, finally having someone on his side, for the first time he wanted to explore his past...

With her.

Bastiano cared for no one and had been raised not to do so, yet he knew now the real reason he was back in Rome.

Sophie.

Maybe the return of his mother's ring was a sign that things were starting to turn around. For the first time he believed that maybe, just maybe there was more to life than revenge.

He walked out and looked over to the table where he had placed the ring last night, yet there was no ring there. He had left it there, Bastiano was sure.

In fact, he could remember precisely the moment he had put it down for it had been then he had become aware that Sophie was near.

And he tried not to think that she too might have seen him with it.

He looked at the floor beneath the table.

Unlike the last time he had been here, the room was immaculate and after a few minutes of fruitless search-ing it was very clear that the ring had gone.

He recalled her expression when he had told her they would go out tonight.

Perhaps Sophie had decided that she needed some-thing to wear.

Had she taken some notes from his wallet he would not have cared, but he'd only just got his mother's ring back.

Bastiano was still scanning the floor and the surfaces as he dressed, still going over last night's details in his mind as he pulled on a shirt and impatient fingers did it up, but he didn't even attempt to tuck it in.

And that was how she saw him.

Sophie had just come from the morning's briefing and instead of house duties she was to work in the foyer, ensuring that all surfaces were gleaming, including the brass revolving doors.

It wasn't her favourite job but it was not an unpleasant one. She could observe the guests and chat with Ronaldo the doorman. It was not an easy shift either, for there were many lounges and there were always guests leaving coffee rings and crumbs. But today she could have been anywhere, she was so happy.

They had shared something so precious last night, Sophie knew it.

And then she saw him and it was not the Bastiano she knew.

Immaculately dressed or deliciously naked, she knew only those two.

Now he looked dishevelled, his clothes thrown on, his shirt barely done up and he wasn't even wearing shoes.

'Sophie…'

His hair was tousled, his jaw unshaven but most disconcerting was his impatience, for she could feel it as he strode up to her.

'Can we speak?'

'I can't.' She tried to smile and address him as if he were just another guest. 'Bastiano, not here…'

'Yes, here!' His voice was low but so clipped that Ronaldo and a couple of guests turned their heads. 'Do you have something of mine?'

'Bastiano…' She was nervous. His eyes were blazing, his lips were pale and tense and she could feel his anger. 'I don't know what you're talking about.'

'Just give it back now and we'll say no more about it.'

Yes, he got that he had never paid her, and he got that she probably thought she deserved something after two nights in a rich man's bed but, hell, *not his ring*!

'Problem?'

Inga perked up and came over. Sophie found she was holding a tense breath but she forced herself to speak. 'No, there's no problem.'

'Sophie...' Bastiano was livid, even his scar seemed to be jumping to the pulse in his cheek, but he waited until Inga had turned around before he spoke again. 'Give me back the ring.'

'I don't know what you're talking about, Bastiano,' Sophie said, relieved that Inga had walked off. 'Can we please speak when my shift ends?'

Only Inga had not merely drifted off but had fetched Benita, the head of housekeeping.

'Can I help you, Signor Conti?' Benita asked.

'It's nothing,' Bastiano said, and he did all he could to rein his temper in. This was her job after all.

But things were already out of hand.

'Signor Conti seems to think that Sophie might have his ring,' Inga said.

'I am sure there is a misunderstanding.' Benita smiled. 'Did you drop it?' She looked around the foyer. 'It might already have been handed in.'

'No, I didn't *drop* it,' Bastiano answered curtly with his eyes firmly fixed on Sophie. 'I'll go to my suite and check again, I'm sure it must be there.'

'Sophie only prepared your room,' Benita patiently answered. 'You weren't even in residence when she did...' And then her voice trailed off as she looked at Sophie's flaming cheeks and then Bastiano, who had clearly just come from bed. And as realisation hit, Benita's eyes briefly shuttered.

It happened, everyone knew that, but Benita had expected better from her, Sophie knew.

'Could you come to my office, please, Sophie?' Benita smiled at Bastiano. 'I shall get to the bottom of this.'

It was awful.

Occasionally staff were caught stealing and Sophie knew only too well what would happen.

'I have to go through your locker with you, Sophie,' Benita said. 'These are very serious accusations, though I'm not just concerned with theft. Have you had any dealings with Signor Conti since he checked in?'

'I did not take his ring.'

'That doesn't answer my question, Sophie,' Benita said, though Sophie's flaming cheeks had already done just that—of course she had had dealings with him.

'You won't find anything in my locker.'

'Then you won't mind me checking.' Benita was firm. 'And if there is nothing to worry about then you will be more than willing to turn out your pockets for me now.'

Bastiano had decided he would be the one to best deal with this. Although he now had no intention of buying the hotel, Benita didn't know that so he walked into the office, ready to take control, just in time to see Sophie pulling from her pocket his mother's ring.

'I don't know how it got there…' She shook her head at the impossibility and then turned and there was Bastiano. 'I didn't take it,' she pleaded.

'Are you saying that you've never seen this ring before?' Benita checked, though there was a slightly mocking edge to her voice, for the evidence was clear.

'Yes,' Sophie said. 'I've never…' And then she halted for to say she had never seen the ring would be an outright lie. Last night, as she had stood nervous and trembling in the alcove she had, after all, watched as Bastiano sat staring at the small piece of jewellery for the longest time before putting it down.

And he would know that she had seen it.

She turned to him and her eyes implored him to believe her. 'Bastiano, I didn't take it.'

Bastiano said nothing.

He wasn't even disappointed in her.

Instead he was disappointed for *them* and scornful of himself—for a moment there he had started to believe in the possibility of them.

Not now.

'Could you wait outside, Sophie?' Benita said, and though her request was polite her voice was pure ice.

Sophie did as she was told.

She leant up against the wall and heard snatches of the conversation; she heard Benita mention the police and knew he was being asked if he wanted formal charges made.

'No,' Bastiano said, but he could see that Benita was tempted to so he pulled rank. 'It would cause more trouble for me than the ring is worth. I have it back now.' His head was pounding; he did not want to be standing here, speaking with the head of housekeeping, though he did so, for one reason only. 'There is no need for Sophie to lose her job, it was a one-off—'

'Signor Conti,' Benita broke in, 'I think we both know that I have more than one reason to fire Sophie.' She gave him a tight smile. 'You own plenty of establishments yourself, you will know that liaisons between staff and guests are an ongoing issue.' She shook her head. 'I will deal with Sophie and, of course, I shall brief Sultan Alim...'

'There's no need for that.'

But Benita wasn't just cross with Sophie.

She was cross with the very esteemed guest for the havoc his libido had caused.

'Unlike Sophie,' Benita tartly responded, 'I value my

job so I shall deal with things by the book. I trust you accept that from the head of housekeeping?'

'Of course.'

He walked out and there Sophie stood, pale in the face with her back against the wall, but she still met his eyes with confidence.

'If you needed money you should have just said…'

Sophie hurt.

Unbearably.

'I was never there for money, Bastiano,' she said, but he was walking off and that incensed her. 'It was about more than that, you know it was.'

'Please…' He raised one hand and flicked it in the air, dismissing her absolutely. Sophie was incensed.

'Why did you send me flowers for my birthday, then?' she called out.

Bastiano halted and then turned and walked back to her.

She had only ever known him nice.

Oh, she'd been warned he could be otherwise, but the Bastiano that other people painted so darkly was one she had never seen.

Until now.

'Your birthday?' He frowned. 'Who said anything about your birthday? I sent flowers so you would know I was in residence and would know to come to my suite. Accordingly, you did.'

Bastiano waited—for an angry slap perhaps, or for Sophie to tell him that she'd always known what a bastard he was, and how he had finally proved it.

Her words cut far deeper though.

'I don't believe you,' Sophie said. 'You're better than that.'

Benita came out then. 'I've got this from here, thank you, Signor Conti.'

She waited until he had walked off and then turned to Sophie.

'Signor Conti doesn't want the police brought in, but I'm left with no choice but to fire you.'

Benita was not cruel in her dismissal—her disappointment was the part that hurt Sophie the most.

'I didn't steal the ring.'

'Sophie, what were you doing to even give him the opportunity to think that you had? We serviced the room and left together, long before Signor Conti arrived.'

She had no answer to that.

'I thought you were better than that,' Benita said. 'It would be bad enough with any guest, but he is the future owner of this very hotel.'

'I didn't know that when we first—'

'So there were other times?' Benita said, and shook her head. 'Come on.'

It was not a pleasant morning.

Her room pass was handed over as well as her uniform. All she had in her locker were some shorts and a strappy top. Having dressed, she emptied it out entirely.

'You had a good job here,' Benita told her. 'You know what this industry is like and how word spreads. You will struggle to find work in a good hotel…'

It was true.

Everything Benita said was true.

But as scared and upset as she was, that was not what hurt.

It was the look he had given her, the black smile that had told her he had expected no less.

No trial by jury.

There wasn't even a trial.

Dario, the head of security, had been summoned and she did not get to leave by the trade door but was escorted out the front to serve as a warning to all staff what happened if caught.

And Bastiano saw it all unfold. He watched as the staff on Reception, the doorman and the maids all paused and turned to watch a rather dignified Sophie walk out.

'Sophie,' Anya called out. 'Your flowers...'

And she almost crumpled.

Sophie looked at the perfect blooms and remembered the joy in her heart when she had received them, and then she glanced over to where he stood. 'I wish I'd never laid eyes on them,' she said, while meeting his dark gaze.

'Likewise,' Bastiano mouthed for her eyes only.

He headed up to his suite but everything he touched turned black. He thought of her, feisty and sunny and smiling when they had met, and how much she had loved her job.

And now she had been fired.

He looked at the ring in his palm and it felt as if it scalded his skin; he was pocketing it when there was a knock at the door.

'Room service.'

Not the type he wanted.

It was Inga with breakfast, and she lifted a silver dome and offered to serve.

'No.'

'Would you like—?'

'Out!' he barked, and when the door closed he picked up the dome himself and saw those bloody baked eggs he had ordered last night while, yes, secretly hoping for Sophie.

He hurled the plate and it slid down the wall.

No, there were no rock stars in residence at the Grande

Lucia, but when the staff came to service the room a few hours later and saw how it had been trashed, it was decided that there might just as well have been.

CHAPTER TEN

THANKFULLY HER FLATMATES were at work when Sophie arrived home and she was able to let go of the tears she had been holding back.

Yesterday had been the happiest day of her life.

Today felt like the worst.

For three months Sophie had lived with the knowledge that she might lose her job over what had happened between her and Bastiano. But the scenario had evolved in the most humiliating, painful way imaginable. And still she had no explanation for how the ring had got into the pocket of her uniform.

She had been branded a thief and a whore, not just by her boss and peers but by Bastiano himself.

Worse, though, even worse was the damning look in his eyes—almost as if he had expected nothing less from her.

It had been her first glimpse of the man that everyone said he was—ruthless and cold—but it was not the Bastiano she knew.

As Sophie stripped off her clothes and pulled on a T-shirt in which to sleep, she flicked out her hair and felt something knotted amongst the strands.

A flower.

The stem was bent and twisted, yet somehow the tiny bloom was still perfect.

Recalling his words—how the flowers had been left to let her know that he was in residence—Sophie was tempted to screw up the rose and toss it into the trash, yet she could not.

It was all she had left of them, the only tangible reminder of a time when life had felt very close to perfect. And so, instead of discarding it, Sophie put it in her journal, pressing the pages together and then placing the journal under her mattress and doing what little she could to preserve the fleeting beauty.

Things did not look any better in the morning.

If anything, in the days ahead, things started to look considerably worse.

The Grande Lucia had been an amazing place to work and Benita was right—getting a job in a hotel of its calibre was going to prove difficult, if not impossible.

The phone calls she made went unanswered or she was told to provide a résumé and references. Sophie knew she had to get to the library and use a computer but even that felt daunting.

'Any luck?' Teresa her flatmate asked when Sophie returned after another fruitless search for work.

'No.' Sophie shook her head. 'Even the cafés aren't hiring.'

Summer really was over.

'You have a message,' Teresa told her, 'from a lady called Bernadetta. She asked you to call her—maybe it is about some work?'

Bernadetta?

Sophie frowned as she read the message and then made the call. Bernadetta was Gabi's boss and the one who had run her ragged in the ballroom that night.

Maybe she had heard and was calling to offer her work.

It was a futile hope and a very fleeting one because two minutes into the conversation it became apparent that Bernadetta had indeed heard the news about Sophie being fired and was speaking to her only because she had to.

'Sultan Alim has asked me to contact you,' she explained tersely. 'I told him that I'm not sure you can be trusted with something so confidential but he insisted.'

'I don't understand.'

'Matrimoni di Bernadetta has been asked to organise his wedding.'

'His wedding? Who is he marrying?'

'Gabi. She just doesn't know that yet.'

Sophie stood there gripping the phone, completely stunned.

'Gabi?' Sophie checked, but Bernadetta had already moved on.

'The wedding is to be this Saturday at the Grande Lucia. As Gabi's close friend, the Sultan wants you there. He also needs you to ensure that Gabi is home on Saturday when he calls her.'

'She doesn't know?'

'It's a surprise.'

Sophie's heart was beating terribly fast. Gabi, *her* Gabi was about to be proposed to by Alim. 'Does that mean Alim is Lucia's father?'

But Bernadetta wasn't calling for a chat. 'Are you prepared to ensure that Gabi is home on Saturday?' she asked.

'I'll do my best,' Sophie said, her head spinning as Bernadetta relayed instructions. Alim, it would seem, had thought of everything, even down to providing an outfit for Sophie that was suitable for a royal wedding.

'You are to go and see Rosa. She is making Gabi's dress, and will put something together for you as well.'

'Rosa?' Sophie swallowed. Rosa might be a friend of Gabi's but her designs were completely out of Sophie's league.

'It's all covered,' Bernadetta practically whistled through gritted teeth. 'If there are any problems please let me know and I must reiterate that you are to say nothing to Gabi.'

'Of course I shan't.'

It was the most exciting, breathtaking, happy news and there was no one to share it with.

First she called Gabi who, after offering her commiserations about Sophie losing her job, then asked if there was anything she could do to help.

'Could you help with my résumé?' Sophie asked. 'I don't have a computer and I tried at the library but I don't know how to make margins.'

'Of course. Come on over.'

'I'll come on Saturday,' Sophie said, and then she remembered something. 'I have to go to the doctor's at nine, I'll come after that.'

It wasn't a lie. Sophie did indeed have to go to the doctor's for a prescription for her Pill. With a royal wedding to go to on Saturday, she rather wished she had been a little bit more organised and had some more Pills so that she could avoid having her period that day!

The wedding should prove a wonderful diversion from her current problems but her heart felt heavier with each passing day. Even walking into an exclusive boutique for a private fitting, it was an effort to smile.

Still, her smile did come a little more readily as Sophie found herself for once spoiled for choice.

'This one would be perfect on you,' Rosa said as she held up a dress that seemed little more than a slip.

It was a gorgeous silver-grey and it actually reminded her of Bastiano's eyes.

'Try it on,' Rosa said. 'And slip on the shoes so you get the full effect.'

Sophie went into a very lavish changing room and pulled off her skirt and top and then tried to put the dress on over her head before discovering a concealed zip.

'Is it on?' Rosa asked.

The dress was amazing. It hung beautifully and gave Sophie curves when she usually had none, but for Sophie there was a concern.

'Isn't it a bit much for a wedding?' she asked as she stepped out, but Rosa had thought of that.

'Indeed, but I have a light overdress that goes well with it in a sheer chiffon. I'll just get it. What size shoe do you take?'

Sophie told her and, left alone, she lifted her hair and was trying to decide whether she should wear her hair up or down when she turned and looked at her silhouette.

She had a bust.

Oh, there was no doubt that Rosa was a miracle worker with fabric but there was also no denying that her small bust was a touch fuller.

It was because of the Pill, Sophie told herself.

'Here,' Rosa said, holding out a sheath of pale fabric that Sophie slipped on over the dress before adding the shoes. It was gorgeous and worked amazingly well, although it did dim the beauty of the dress just a fraction. 'You look wonderful.' Rosa smiled. 'I cannot wait to see Gabi's face when she finds out all that Alim has arranged.'

'Are there many guests?' Sophie asked a little later as, for the first time in her life and long overdue, she splurged on some gorgeous underwear.

'Just family and close friends.'

It was her first inkling that Bastiano might be there. Sophie knew that he and Alim were friends.

She watched as Rose wrapped her new silver knickers and lacy bra in tissue paper, and Sophie vowed to herself that Bastiano wouldn't be seeing them.

Yet, though the thought of seeing him would usually have consumed her, Sophie awoke on the morning of the wedding with more than the possibility of seeing Bastiano on her mind.

In the bathroom, having showered, she tried to quash the gnawing of anxiety in her stomach, for her period still had not arrived.

Stress can delay things, Sophie told herself.

Not that she really knew, but she had heard it said amongst friends, and so at her appointment at the doctor's that morning she suggested the same.

The doctor just handed her a jar.

'I've taken my Pill every day,' Sophie said when she returned with her specimen and the doctor ran the test.

'Do you take it on time?'

'Always…' Sophie said, and then swallowed as she thought back to the other morning when she had been fired. 'I had an upset the other day, I might not have taken it until lunchtime.'

'The other day?' The doctor frowned. 'Sophie, you are pregnant.'

'I don't think so.' Sophie shook her head. She had come here to be reassured, to be told she was mad to worry, but the doctor just looked at Sophie as the news started to sink in. 'I can't be.'

As the doctor examined her Sophie's fear only increased.

'I would say that you're more than twelve weeks.'

'How could I not know?' She started to cry, but this doctor was far kinder than the one back home and took some time to gently explain that not all women had symptoms.

'People have commented that my uniform was getting tight,' Sophie said. 'I just never gave it much thought.'

It was a lot to take in, an awful lot to take in, and Sophie left the doctor's more bewildered than she had ever been in her life.

But she had to get to Gabi's.

'Hey.' Gabi gave her a smile and then when she saw Sophie's puffy eyes she drew her inside. 'You'll get another job.'

'I loved that one, though,' Sophie said. It was easier to let Gabi think that her tears were about losing her job and Gabi soon set to work, typing up her friend's résumé.

'You really need a reference,' Gabi said. 'Why don't you put me? I can say you've helped me organise some weddings.'

'That's stretching it,' Sophie sighed.

'Well, why don't you put me as a personal one for now?'

Gabi made it all look so easy, and soon she had printed off several copies of Sophie's résumé, but as she handed them over, curiosity got the better of Gabi and she asked what Sophie had been doing in Bastiano's room.

'Oh.' Sophie was immediately on the defensive. 'So now you think I stole his ring?'

'Of course not!'

'I would never steal,' Sophie said. 'But if I did, I would not steal some stupid emerald and pearl ring. It would be diamonds.'

Gabi laughed and just as she did the phone rang and she went to answer it. Sophie watched as her friend's face paled and she excused herself and went into the bedroom.

It must be Alim!

A few minutes later Gabi emerged, declaring that she had a migraine.

'That came on quickly,' Sophie said as she was ushered out.

'Yes, they tend to.'

They promised to catch up soon but as Sophie walked off, though happy for her friend she felt terribly lonely too. Gabi had struggled with being a single mother, yet she had a job and her mother lived here in Rome.

And now she had Alim.

Sophie couldn't help but wonder what hope there was for her when she had none of those things.

She had nothing, save for her Sicilian pride, though even that was going to be hard to find today.

Sophie tried, though.

She got ready and she wore make-up through necessity rather than choice. Just a little, but enough to ensure that no one could guess she'd been crying. And for once she wore her hair down, though more because it would hopefully hide some of her blushes when she walked into the hotel.

The dress was a dream but, now that Sophie knew she was pregnant, it seemed terribly obvious, for her bust was certainly fuller and there was a soft curve to her stomach. Sophie was very grateful to add to her outfit the sheer fabric that hid even a tell-tale hint that her body had changed.

And so to the Grande Lucia.

She took a cab, which was a treat in itself for Sophie, and as it pulled up Ronaldo jumped forward to let the passenger out.

'*Benvenuto...*' he said, but then Ronaldo's warm welcome petered out as he realised who it was, and now his greeting was both awkward and curt. 'Sophie.'

'Ronaldo.'

She climbed out of the cab and took a second to seemingly fiddle with her dress, though really she was trying to summon the courage to walk inside.

Through the brass revolving doors she went and into the familiar foyer.

It didn't feel familiar, though, for instead of hearing her name called and the regular smiles and waves as she walked through, her ex-colleagues all pretended to be busy and looked the other way.

All that she could handle, Sophie thought as she stood outside the ballroom and gave her name.

The sly glances and whispers, and even being downright ignored, all hurt, but it was a manageable hurt.

What her heart couldn't deal with, though, as she walked through the entrance doors of the ballroom, was the certain knowledge that Bastiano was here.

Even without sighting him, Sophie knew that he was.

There was a current that ran through her whenever he was close and she could feel his eyes on her as she again gave her name so that she could be guided to her seat.

He was here, she was certain.

Yes, Bastiano was there.

He had withdrawn his offer for the hotel and would gladly never have set foot in the place again, yet business was business, he had told Alim.

And they were still friends.

So, having offered his best wishes to the surprisingly nervous groom, he was just taking his seat as they awaited the arrival of the bride when Sophie appeared.

She looked stunning, Bastiano thought.

He watched Sophie momentarily falter as she was guided to the seats near his.

'I am a friend of the bride,' she said to the woman who was ushering her towards where he sat. 'I should be on the other side.'

But this was no ordinary wedding, and she went where she was guided, away from the side where all the royalty had been seated.

'We commoners sit together,' Sophie said as she took her place beside him and Bastiano gave a tight smile.

'For now,' he responded, looking ahead rather than at her.

As soon as the service was over he would move away, Bastiano decided. She might just as well have spilled a bottle of perfume over herself for her fragrance overwhelmed him, yet he knew she had not. The scent was pure Sophie and for now he had to breathe it in, aware of every flicker as she sat supremely still beside him.

And then as the ballroom doors opened they stood and Sophie turned, seeing her friend but all the time feeling Bastiano's eyes boring into the back of her head.

'You knew!' Gabi mouthed as she caught sight of her, and Sophie smiled for her friend; as Alim kissed little Lucia, Sophie did her level best not to break down.

She wanted to tell Bastiano about the baby, she wanted there to be hope for them.

But there was none.

There never had been, she now knew.

It had never been going to end well.

She wanted to be happy for her friend, yet to stand broken-hearted at a wedding, next to the man who had shattered her happiness, was a very private hell and too much to sustain.

Gabi and Alim were in love, it was plain to see.

It just seemed to magnify the hopelessness of her situation as she stood next to Bastiano.

'How long does the service go on for?' he asked at one point.

'How the hell would I know?' Sophie responded and she felt rather than heard his slight mirthless laugh.

It truly was agony.

Finally, though, Gabi and Alim were husband and wife.

As the chairs were moved away and the guests went to take their seats at the tables for the celebratory meal Sophie looked at the place cards and saw she would be seated by him.

It was a hell she chose not to sustain.

'Gabi…' She kissed her friend and congratulated her and then she struggled how best to say what she had to.

Gabi said it for her. 'You're going to go?'

'I just…'

She felt sick.

Oh, maybe it was all in her head and simply because she knew she was pregnant, but suddenly she felt light-headed and nauseous and utterly out of place.

'I understand, Sophie,' Gabi said, for she had heard all the rumours and could have thought of nothing worse than being forced to sit next to Alim when her own world had fallen apart.

'I'm so happy for you,' Sophie said. 'I honestly am. I wouldn't have missed the wedding for the world.'

It was the reception that she could not tolerate.

'Here.' Gabi swiped Sophie's place card from the table and wrote something down. 'That's Alim's private number. Put him down as a reference.'

'I can't.'

'Yes, Sophie, you can.'

'I'll only use it if I'm desperate.'

Desperate was how she felt, though not about work.

She wanted to walk right up to Bastiano and plead her case. She wanted to tap him on the shoulder right now and tell him that she did not take his stupid ring. And she wanted to tell him what she had found out just a few hours ago.

Her eyes scanned the room and immediately she saw him—talking to some leggy blonde. Or rather she was talking as Bastiano's restless eyes scoured the room and found Sophie's.

She turned and walked away and headed for the rest-rooms, but she didn't get that far.

Sophie looked over to Reception, where Anya stood—once they would have chatted, but now Anya could not meet her eyes.

And there was Inga, polishing the brass doors and chatting to Ronaldo.

Everyone ignored her.

Once she had belonged but, like it or not, she no longer did, so Sophie left.

Not just the wedding.

It was time to accept that there was nothing for her here in Rome and to return home.

Her disappearance did not go unnoticed.

'Excuse me,' Bastiano said to the leggy blonde.

He had no idea who the woman was but that was nothing new.

The difference today was that anonymity held no charm.

He wanted to speak to Sophie, to find out how she had fared. He wanted to know that everything was okay in her world and then he could walk away more easily.

Bastiano could not find her.

As he took his seat the place card next to his had gone, though Bastiano being Bastiano had already checked and knew full well that Sophie had been placed next to him.

Perhaps she had asked to be moved, Bastiano decided when the table filled and the space next to him remained empty.

Wise choice, he told himself, though that did not sit right.

But then the lighting dimmed and it became increasingly clear that Sophie hadn't just moved tables, she had left the venue.

'Where's Sophie?' he asked the happy couple, having sat through the meal and endless speeches.

'I expect it got a bit too much for her,' Gabi said, and she looked straight at Bastiano. 'It would be hard to be here, labelled a thief by everyone and the subject of painful gossip. I'm just grateful she made it to the service.'

And later Bastiano could not help but have a word with Alim.

'I think Sophie might have been dealt with a bit harshly.'

'Oh, so you're in the practice of hiring thieves?' Alim asked, raising his brows, but then he saw his friend's concern. 'She'll be okay.'

'She won't get work.'

'Not true. I've just been informed that I'm to act as a reference.'

And with Sultan Alim of Zethlehan as a reference, Sophie would be okay.

Bastiano could relax now and put the unfortunate incident behind him.

Except he couldn't.

There were beautiful guests galore and yet he was in bed before the bride and groom.

Alone.

And he woke, as he always did, before the sun.

'Entra!' he called, when on the dot of six his breakfast was delivered and he closed his eyes to indicate he did not want conversation.

Some things never changed.

Except they had.

'Would you like me to serve?'

He opened his eyes to the pale blue ones of Inga, the maid that Sophie did not like.

'Out,' he told her, and struggled to contain his anger, for Bastiano had worked out what had happened.

It took less than an hour to prove his hunch.

He stood over Dario, with Benita by his side, looking at old CCTV tapes.

'My breakfast is served at six every morning, except on that morning.'

'You ordered it for seven,' Benita said, looking at the paperwork.

'No.'

Of that he was certain.

The only variance to his breakfast order had been the occasional *shakshuka* and that had either been eaten by a sexy maid or flung against the wall.

His breakfast was always at six.

There it was, right on time, being delivered by Inga.

And there it was, not two minutes later, being wheeled back out.

Sophie was not a thief.

Most disconcerting to Bastiano, though, was that he

had cared enough to find out and pursue justice for his little maid.

'She will get her job back now?' Bastiano checked, but Benita gave an uncomfortable shrug.

'Sophie wasn't just fired for stealing.'

'If turning tricks is the criteria for firing maids at the Grande Lucia,' Bastiano responded tartly, 'then the unemployment rate in Rome is about to skyrocket. Would you like me to name names?'

Benita closed her eyes for a moment before responding. 'That shan't be necessary.'

'Good,' Bastiano retorted! 'So you will be rehiring Sophie?' Bastiano checked, and Benita nodded.

An hour later Bastiano boarded his helicopter for home with his conscience clear.

Almost.

Not.

CHAPTER ELEVEN

SOPHIE HATED HER JOB.

She tried not to show it, of course.

But no matter how thoroughly she cleaned the sleazy bar on the edge of her home town, the surfaces did not gleam and the carpets were still sticky.

Still, Sophie far preferred the cleaning duty when the bar was closed to the hours when it was open.

It was a job and a roof over her head, she told herself, though not for much longer. Pino, her boss, had made it clear when he'd hired her that the live-in post was a temporary one. Now, at six months pregnant, she was still no closer to working out where she would live when the baby arrived.

It would not be at her parents'.

Sophie had left home in disgrace, returned in shame, and after a lot of heartache they had asked the priest to speak with her. She had been told of couples who were desperate for a baby and would be able to provide a wonderful home.

An argument had ensued when Sophie had told her family that she would be the one to provide for her baby and she had barely seen them since.

Gabi's mother might have come around once little

Lucia had arrived, but Sophie knew that it would not be the case with her own parents.

And she could not stay there.

Even if Pino did keep her on, she wouldn't want to raise her baby in a room over a bar such as this.

And Pino gave her the creeps.

Which was why, instead of, as she usually did, working through her rare day off, Sophie headed upstairs to her small bedroom.

'Where are you going?' Pino asked. 'It's time to open up.'

'It's my day off,' Sophie reminded him.

'Well, I need you to work.' Pino shrugged and went to open the main door, clearly not expecting a discussion.

'I have an appointment in town today,' Sophie said, 'at the hospital. It's my six-month check. I cannot miss it.'

It was a lie.

Sophie had had just a couple of visits to her old family doctor but she didn't tell Pino that. Instead, she headed upstairs and washed as best she could in the small bathroom she shared with Pino and then pulled on a black dress and boots and a thin jacket.

As she came down the stairs she could hear Pino chatting to one of the regulars and hoped she could slip out unnoticed.

'Sophie!'

Just as she got to the door he called out to her.

'Make sure you're back for five.'

That would be pushing it.

Casta was three hours away and three back, and she had no idea how long it would take to get to the Old Convent from the railway station, or how long the interview would take.

For the first time in months she had hope.

A woman who dropped off some deliveries to the bar had told her about the Old Convent in Casta. It was an upmarket health and wellness facility and they were look-ing for live-in chambermaids.

'It's gorgeous,' she told Sophie. 'They take only the best produce...' She sneered in the direction of Pino. 'He takes the dregs. You should call them. A woman called Karmela runs the housekeeping. My niece worked there. They took her on when she was pregnant and she carried on working there for two years after the baby was born.'

'She lived there with the baby?' Sophie's heart had started thumping so fast it must have woken her own baby up because she felt its little kicks.

'Yes. She worked hard, mind you, but she loved it. Look your neatest, though, it's very posh.'

The telephone interview had gone very well and now, as the train went through a tunnel, Sophie dug in her bag and found a comb.

Oh, she would love to make more of an effort, Sophie thought, but she had nothing to make an effort with.

She did have Alim's number!

Sophie took the place card from the wedding out of her purse and looked at it for a long moment.

She hadn't used it yet. The type of jobs that she had been able to find had not required a reference, certainly not one from a sultan, and she would not use this gift lightly.

Yet she needed it today.

Sophie couldn't wait to meet her baby, but she was no-where ready to. Her parents' suggestion of adoption had very quickly taught Sophie just how much she wanted her baby.

Yes, the circumstances were far from ideal, but her baby was already much loved.

The train pulled out of the tunnel and into the belly of the valley of Casta. It was the first time she had ever been there and the scenery was breath-taking. Ahead was the ocean, with a hill either side of the valley, and now the train turned seemingly on a dime and ran on stilted tracks that hugged the rocky hillside.

Sophie dared not look down so she closed her eyes and rested her head against the window.

She should have stayed in Rome, Sophie thought. At least there she had had friends.

She ached to contact Gabi but did not know what to say—after all, her friend was now married to royalty. Would it sound as if she was begging for help when she told her she was pregnant?

But it wasn't just that.

Alim was a friend of Bastiano's.

With the best will in the world Sophie knew that Gabi would be worried if she found out her predicament and would end up telling Alim.

Would he tell Bastiano?

Sophie guessed that eventually he would and Bastiano's reaction to the news…

Sophie did not want to know.

Oh, he would be aggrieved and cross and no doubt decide she had set out to trap him.

His anger she could deal with.

Almost.

What she couldn't cope with, though, was the sense of duty that would surely ensue.

Bastiano was right—they were the same.

Beneath the glamour of his life, beneath the fearsome reputation and his playboy ways, he was as Sicilian as she.

Bastiano Conti forced into a duty marriage was something that Sophie could not bear to think of.

She had run from one after all.

As she stepped out of the train Sophie breathed in the salty air; the wind whipped her hair and she pulled her jacket tighter.

'I am looking for the Old Convent,' Sophie told a woman behind the station desk, and she was informed that there was a bus due in fifteen minutes.

'Though it only takes you to the base.'

Sophie nodded. She had been told on the phone that there was a gated entrance and once she arrived she had been told to buzz and a car would be sent to collect her.

The bus took her through Casta and then inched its way up the hill, but Sophie was too nervous to take in the view. She was let off, seemingly in the middle of nowhere, but Karmela's instructions were good and soon she pressed a buzzer on the gate and gave her name and said she was there for an interview.

Soon a car arrived and she was driven down a long driveway with overhanging trees on either side, and then they arrived at the Old Convent building.

The grounds were sumptuous. There were fountains and pretty walkways and, far from foreboding, as she stepped into Reception there was a tranquil air to the old building.

'Sophie?' The receptionist was friendly and greeted her by name. After filling in a few forms, she was shown through to her interview.

Karmela, the head of housekeeping, greeted her and asked her to take a seat, wasting no time before getting the interview under way.

'You said on the phone that you had experience in a five-star hotel.'

'I worked at the Grande Lucia in Rome for a year.'

'Can I ask why you left?'

Sophie told the truth.

In part.

'I had some issues with my baby's father.'

'Well, he would have trouble creating issues here. The security is tight, there is limited access and it is gated.'

It wasn't that type of trouble Sophie had been having, of course, but she gave Karmela a smile.

'You would have to sign a confidentiality clause. Some of our guests are very famous and we do not want staff speaking out of turn.'

'We had many famous and titled guests at the Grande Lucia.'

'I understand that.' Karmela nodded. 'Here, though, a lot of our guests are…' She hesitated. 'Shall we say, recovering from a life lived in the fast lane.'

'Oh.'

'Does that concern you?'

'Not at all,' Sophie said.

'You're currently working?' Karmela asked as she read through her paperwork.

Sophie had updated it by hand.

'I am.'

'Would you be happy for me to ring for a reference?'

Sophie's throat went dry and it took a moment before she could respond. 'I think that might make things rather awkward for me.'

'How much notice would he require?' Karmela asked, and she looked up from the paperwork at Sophie and watched as she struggled to reply.

Oh, she did not know how best to put it. 'He would not take it well if I told him I was leaving.'

Karmela seemed to get it immediately.

'What about your previous role?'

'Sultan Alim is my reference—he's the owner of the Grande Lucia. He gave me his private number to use.'

'May I contact him?'

'Of course,' Sophie said, and wrote down the number.

The rest of the interview went very well and soon Karmela was speaking as if Sophie already had the job!

'You will be required to service the rooms and to provide a turndown service. We encourage guests to eat in the restaurant but on occasion you would also be required to deliver meals to their suites. Some of our guests can be rather demanding, but I am sure you are used to that.'

Sophie nodded and decided that now was the time to address the obvious.

'I know that I might only be able to work for a couple of months, but I am very good at my job and when I've had my baby I will work harder still.'

'Sophie, we're very used to single mothers here. There is room in the cells for both a bed and a cot.'

'Cells?'

'We have kept the names of old. The cells are where the nuns would sleep but don't worry, they have been modernised. They are basic but very comfortable. In your case the timing works well—there's a two-month period where you'll be entirely supernumerary and trained to our standard. Signor Conti has a very strict vision for the place that has worked well...'

'Signor Conti?'

'Sì.' Karmela nodded. 'Bastiano Conti. His facilities are world renowned. This gorgeous old building was a dilapidated shell when he first bought it. Now guests fly in from all over the world to retreat here...'

Sophie didn't hear the rest of what was said.

The Old Convent was owned by Bastiano.

There was no way she could work here now, Sophie thought as hope was snatched away.

As soon as he saw that she was pregnant...

Sophie closed her eyes as she pictured Bastiano finding out that the thieving maid who had delivered far more than breakfast was now pregnant with his child.

Sophie simply could not bear to face it.

She was too busy trying not to break down as Karmela wound up the interview.

'The driver will take you directly to the train station,' Karmela told her as she saw her to a waiting car. 'I'll be in touch soon.'

Karmela was as good as her word and the following morning Sophie took a call informing her that the role was hers.

To both women's regret Sophie politely declined.

CHAPTER TWELVE

'*Buon Compleanno!*'

'*Grazie,*' Bastiano responded mechanically as his PA wished him a happy birthday.

She was new and from out of town and, of course, did not know that there was no such thing as a happy birthday for Bastiano.

It had been the day his mother had died after all.

He rather hoped she would leave things there, but given that he had been gone for a few days there was much to catch up on.

'How was your meeting in Rome?' she asked.

'Fine.'

He had been back three times since the wedding and though he was no longer vying to purchase the Grande Lucia, he had told his PA to book him in there on business.

Certainly there had been no pleasure.

Rome had felt empty.

There was no sign of Sophie and, given all that had happened, he had been loath to enquire as to her whereabouts.

Bastiano did his best to ignore the date and dealt with the essentials, but by lunchtime he gave in and pressed on the intercom.

'Call for my car.'

A short while later he drove down the private road he had had built when he had taken over the convent and headed into the small town.

He parked by the church and walked down the gravelly side to the graveyard.

He came here rarely now.

He had used to visit Maria's grave, more out of guilt than grief, but he was not here to visit Maria today.

As a child, he would visit his mother's grave on certain occasions, but there were no memories to draw on and there had never been any comfort to be had.

Again, there was none today.

Just guilt.

He had been raised on it.

It was a pervasive guilt that time did not ease, for his very existence had robbed her of life.

Logic tried to tell him otherwise.

His mother had told no one about the baby she carried, and had done all she could to avoid showing—skipping meals until she had fainted one day. She had arrived at the convent hungry and weak.

The Old Convent might no longer be consecrated but for Bastiano those rules of old still applied, hence the policy of support to single mothers who wished to work there.

If only his mother had gone there sooner.

'I have your ring,' he told her, but there was no sudden rustle in the trees and the birds sang just as they had before.

There was no sign that she had heard.

He took it from his pocket and thought back to when Raul had come to visit to ask for Lydia's address, and the opportunity had arisen to ask for the one thing that was precious to him.

It did not feel so precious now.

He stared at the emerald and the tiny seed pearls but instead of beauty he saw only its curse.

Both of the women he'd loved had been wearing it when they had died.

And then he thought of Sophie, turning out her pockets and holding it in her palm, along with the cruel words he had hurled at her.

Of course the flowers had been for her birthday; at the time it had felt easier to lie than admit to caring.

He had lost her for this ring.

What once had been vital was meaningless now. Bastiano took the small ring and tossed it, for it had brought no peace; all it signified was destruction and pain.

He had to know for himself how she was.

Bastiano simply had to know that Sophie was doing okay.

He was the *stulto* now as he drove back up the hill, for he took the bends far too fast and was impatient at the gate, leaving his car with the engine still running.

'Park it,' he told the doorman.

Through the convent he strode, and before he could change his mind he delivered instructions.

'I want to speak with Sultan Alim,' Bastiano said. 'I'll take the call in my office.

'Of course.'

Zethlehan was three hours ahead of Sicily but even though it was late afternoon there Bastiano knew it might take some time to be put through as Alim would likely be busy.

It wasn't Alim he wanted to speak to, though, but Gabi.

Bastiano just had to know how Sophie was.

It felt as if it was taking for ever to get hold of Alim.

He paced his office and looked out at the view of the strait but it did nothing to soothe him, as it usually it did.

At seventeen, when Maria's will had been read, he had scaled the convent walls just to get away from the toxic gossip in the village.

As Raul had started his ascent in Rome, Bastiano had remained in Casta.

His rise had been slower than Raul's.

Bastiano had seen the potential of the building and his low offer had been accepted; he had taken a loan and renovations had commenced.

The first clients had trickled in and then a B-list actor had moaned to the press about the cost, saying that it was prohibitive.

In response to the best publicity he could have hoped for, Bastiano had tripled the rates.

Now there was a waiting list to get in, though they kept two places on constant reserve should a young royal or such need urgent respite.

Though he had several more exclusive retreats under his belt this was his base and served as his platform to the world. Thanks to his famous guests, Bastiano was a name on the most coveted guest lists. He travelled frequently and partied hard but it was here that he chose to return.

Yet lately these walls no longer felt like home.

'I have Sultan Alim on the line.'

Bastiano picked up the phone.

'How are you?' Alim asked.

'I am well,' Bastiano said. 'Very well. Have you sold that hotel yet?'

'It is off the market,' Alim replied. 'Why, have you changed your mind?'

'No.' Bastiano was rarely awkward. 'Actually, I was

hoping to have a word with Gabi. I wondered if she had heard anything from Sophie.'

'Sophie?'

'The chambermaid...'

'I know who she is. I thought you were back in touch.'

'Why would you think that?'

'Because your head of housekeeping called a while back for a reference. I gave her a glowing one.'

Sophie had been here?

Bastiano made a few noises and said a few words but in less than a minute he had ended the call. He rang Reception and asked that Karmela meet him in his office.

All this time he had been worrying and wondering, only to find out that Sophie had passed through.

'Is anything wrong?' Karmela asked, looking worried as she came in.

'Nothing is wrong,' Bastiano said. 'You interviewed a young woman a couple of months ago...'

'I interview many people.'

'Sophie,' he said. 'She used to work at the Grande Lucia.'

'Ah, yes.'

'She wasn't offered the position?' he checked.

'Indeed she was. Sophie was an excellent candidate and her references checked out, but when I rang to offer her the job she said that she had accepted another position.'

'Where?'

'I didn't ask that,' Karmela said. 'I was disappointed and also cross that she had wasted so much time. I had even told her that there would be no problem when the baby came...'

'Baby?'

'You have always said that so long as their children are kept out of earshot you don't mind if we employ single mothers.'

'I meant, are you saying she was pregnant?'

'Yes, about five or six months along,' Karmela recalled. 'She said she'd had to get out of Rome because she was having some issues with the baby's father.'

The words were like knives.

'Bring me her résumé.'

He was sweating.

Even in the blistering heat of a Sicilian summer Bastiano was so fit that he barely broke a sweat. Even when held by the throat by Raul and accused of causing the death of Maria, he'd stayed cool.

Not now.

He cast his mind back to the wedding and the last time he had seen her. If what Karmela was saying was correct, then Sophie would have been about three months pregnant then.

He would have known. They had made love the night before!

Yet the fast, frantic sex had been the result of pure need and as for the morning...

Karmela brought him the paperwork and though Bastiano wanted to be alone, there were questions he needed to ask.

Most of it was typewritten but her most recent employment was written by hand.

'What is this address?'

'A bar, and not a particularly nice one,' Karmela said. 'I didn't bother to ring them for a reference.'

'Why not?'

'Sophie told me it was a live-in job but she didn't feel particularly comfortable there and it would be made worse if her boss knew that she was considering leaving. I rang her previous employer instead, Sultan Alim.'

Bastiano waved his hand to dismiss her, for he needed to digest all he had just been told, but as she reached the door there was something he had to know, something that could not be gleaned from the pages he held in his hand.

'How did she look?'

Karmela held out her hands and gave a somewhat helpless shrug, unsure what to say. 'Signor Conti, it was a couple of months ago…'

'How did she look?' he asked again. Bastiano did not care if his questions led Karmela to think that the baby was his, for his only concern now was Sophie.

'Tired,' Karmela said.

'And?' Bastiano pushed.

Karmela thought for a moment. 'Relieved. She seemed terribly relieved to have found this place. I got the distinct impression she was struggling where she was, which was why I was so surprised when she turned down the job.'

And Bastiano knew why she had.

Sophie had thought him wonderful when they'd first met—a gentleman who would not have her leave his suite in wet clothes.

She had seen only the good in him.

Until he had proved himself to be otherwise.

In the throes of love making she had pleaded for him never to let her down and he had.

It was time, Bastiano knew, to put things right.

'It's time to open up,' Pino called as he rapped loudly on Sophie's bedroom door.

'I'll be right there.'

It was late on a rainy afternoon and she was exhausted and had a headache to boot.

Lately she had been unable to sleep. She was simply too uncomfortable or too nervous with Pino prowling around, but this afternoon the baby was asleep and Sophie wanted to close her eyes and join it.

It wasn't an option, though.

She hauled herself from the bed and pulled on her shoes. Running a brush through her hair, she braced herself for another long shift behind the bar and then cleaning glasses late into the night.

Sophie knew only too well she could not work for much longer. The baby was not due for another six weeks but her body was telling her that she needed to rest.

Where, though?

She had been so defiant when she had told her parents and the priest that she would provide for her baby but the truth was she had saved little. Her job covered board and meals but the wages after that were tiny.

As she walked out of the bedroom, there in the hallway was Pino.

He gave her the creeps the way he was always hanging around.

'I've been thinking,' he said as she headed down the stairs and he walked behind her. 'You're a good worker, perhaps you can stay on once the baby comes.'

'Stay on?' she turned at the bottom of the stairs and for a second, maybe two, she actually thought that Pino was being nice as he moved past her and unbolted the door.

'You can move your things into the front bedroom at the weekend. It's warmer there.'

It was the middle of January, and not cold as such, but it was wet and the building was damp—though it was not for that reason that Pino would have Sophie move her things.

The front bedroom was his.

Never.

But now the fight was over.

Sophie knew she would have to contact Bastiano.

Oh, she was more than aware that it took two to make a baby and he had responsibilities.

It was the extent to which he might meet them that broke her heart.

Sophie walked into the bar as the patrons trickled in. She knew most of their orders without asking, which was just as well for her mind was too busy for conversation.

Sophie knew that she had to leave.

And soon.

'Sophie!' Her name was being called from several directions and she poured their drinks but did not serve them with a smile.

There was an impatient drumming of fingers coming from the left.

He could wait.

Sophie had perfected ignoring an impatient patron until she was ready to serve.

'Can I help you?' Sophie finally asked the drumming fingers, yet before she had even looked up she was on high alert.

His nails were neat and manicured and there was an expensive scent that in this place was non-existent rather than rare.

Her eyes slowly lifted, taking in the tie and dark suit, and then she met the eyes she had ached to see yet had sought to avoid.

'Bastiano…'

Her mind was moving slowly, trying to tell her that it was possible that he had been passing by and had just stopped in for a drink, while at the same time knowing this place was light years away from anywhere that he would frequent.

'What can I get you?' she asked.

'I'd like to speak with you in private.'

His olive skin was pale and the scar on his cheek was so livid it looked as if it had been freshly seared into his flesh.

Sophie could taste his fury and she felt her chest constrict as his eyes looked down at her swollen stomach.

What she did not understand was that his fury was not aimed at her.

Bastiano had been observing Pino—standing with his arms folded behind the bar and watching Sophie work. Not only had Pino's laziness incensed Bastiano, he had also seen the roaming of his eyes.

He wanted Sophie out of here.

'I'm working,' she told him, playing for time, for, even after many months preparing for a moment such as this one, still Sophie was none the wiser as to what to say, and so, of course, she said the wrong thing. 'What can I get you?'

'Sophie!' he warned. 'I want to speak to you now, outside.'

'She already told you—she's working.'

Bastiano did not even look over as Pino spoke on. 'I think it's time for you to leave.'

The bar fell silent.

Pino's voice signalled danger and, after all, there was a stranger in town.

A slick, suited stranger and she watched as Pino looked out of the window at Bastiano's rather flash car. It was clear to all that he did not belong here.

'I'm not going anywhere,' Bastiano said, and as he did so he looked right into Sophie's eyes. 'Until we have spoken.'

'Bastiano…' she attempted, and her voice came out a little high and strained. 'Not now.'

She wanted to warn him not to make a scene here, for she had seen more than her share of trouble within these walls.

'You heard her,' Pino said, and then made an already tense situation a hundred times worse for he came over and put an arm around her shoulders.

Sophie shrugged him off but the damage was more than done.

To Sophie, apart from on that terrible morning, Bastiano had always been kind, but she saw the other side to him now.

He did not explode; instead, it was far worse. It was as if the bar had been placed in refrigeration.

She could almost see the white of Bastiano's breath when he spoke for his words were pure ice.

'Sophie,' he said. 'Go and wait in the car.'

She would be angry with Bastiano later.

Right now she simply wanted out.

But she wanted him to follow her out because she knew how rough the bar's patrons could be.

'We'll speak outside,' she suggested.

'No,' Bastiano corrected her, though his eyes never left Pino's face. 'You go and wait in the car and I shall collect your things.'

Bastiano lifted the flap of the bar and Sophie walked out. The patrons parted as the one lady present left; when she was inside his vehicle, with a bleep, Bastiano locked her in safely.

He was angry with good reason for he knew she had been too scared to give this man as a reference.

Bastiano knew *exactly* his type.

Uninvited and most unwelcome, he walked behind the bar and into the hallway.

Pino followed him.

Bastiano climbed the stairs and found the cupboard Pino called a room—and no doubt charged Sophie half her wages to live in.

It took two minutes to clear it.

There was an old wooden wardrobe that held a couple of skirts and a bag that felt like it held some shoes. The chest of drawers contained just as little and Bastiano had soon packed her things. He went into the bathroom and picked up her brush and make-up and pulled down all the underwear that dripped over the bath. Not because Sophie would be needing them, for soon she would have much finer things, more because he could not stand that Pino had seen them.

He went back to the room and looked under the bed and found another pair of shoes and then he lifted the mattress and found her purse and a small leather journal. He had been poor once too, and he knew all the tricks.

'She owes me two weeks' notice.' Pino was at the door, watching his every move.

Bastiano said nothing, but as he stuffed Sophie's belongings into the bag the journal fell open and there, pressed between the pages, was a rose. *His* rose.

'I said…' Pino continued, but that single rose was Bastiano's undoing and he pressed the man against the wall.

'You make me sick,' Bastiano told him, and then he told him something else. 'Lucky for you she has her own room because if I find out you have so much as touched her, I suggest you sleep with one eye open.'

Pino seemed to recognise the ferocity in Bastiano's threat, so he put his hands up and Bastiano let him go.

He walked down the steps and out through bar with her bag over his shoulder; there were many fools present but not one game enough to speak out.

Or rather there was one fool.

From the safety of the top of the steps Pino had the last word.

'At least I gave her shelter. Where were you?'

Sophie watched from the car and she waited for the sound of a fight yet it was all eerily quiet and then, to her confusion, as calm as anything, Bastiano walked out.

He unlocked the car and climbed in, throwing her bag into the back and fighting to contain his temper as Pino's words replayed in his head.

'You had no right to charge in—' Sophie started, but Bastiano broke in.

'Is it my baby?'

'You know it is.'

'Then I had every right.'

He wanted to pull off hard, to leave some rubber in his wake, yet he had never driven with a pregnant woman beside him before. 'Why didn't you come to me?' He didn't get it, he truly did not, and was doing his best to contain his temper as he drove. 'You came to the Old Convent looking for work and yet chose to return here. Why?'

'Because I found out you owned it,' Sophie said. 'I didn't want you to know.'

'Why?' Bastiano demanded, but then gave in. Now was not the time for a row. He wanted her in Casta, he wanted her rested and fed.

'We'll talk back at the Old Convent.'

'What will your staff think when I arrive?'

'I have no idea,' Bastiano said, 'neither do I care.'

'Well, I do,' Sophie retorted, and now she too was angry. 'Are you intent on ruining every job I get?'

'Don't worry, Sophie, you will never have to work again.'

'I never used to worry about going to work,' Sophie said. 'I loved my job.'

She had, Bastiano knew that.

'Why didn't you come to me?' he asked again. 'I know I'm a bastard...'

'I never said you were.'

She hadn't.

They were coming to the stretch of road where he had witnessed Maria's crash.

The convent was visible in the distance as they drove in angry silence.

'It's beautiful,' Sophie commented as they passed a humble little church in golden limestone with a small bell tower.

Bastiano glanced over—pretty certainly wasn't the word that came to his mind as they drove past, for behind the church was the graveyard that held only dark memories for him.

'I'm glad you think so, given we'll be there in a couple of weeks.'

'Excuse me?'

'We should marry before the baby is born...'

Should.

That single word said it all.

She would be his wife by duty and nothing more.

It was the real reason that she had chosen not to tell him and had done her very best to go it alone.

Bastiano was right.

They were the same.

She had known exactly what his response would be.

Sophie looked over at him, a man who, when she'd met him, had been considering marrying a woman he had never even dated.

'You would take more care choosing an apple from the tree than in choosing a wife.'

'I don't pick apples.' Bastiano shrugged. 'They come to me peeled and sliced.'

'You know what I mean.'

The car was approaching the entrance to the convent now and Bastiano did not need to buzz. The gates sensed his car and slowly opened as they approached.

'You don't have to marry me, Bastiano,' Sophie said as the car idled, and she did not meet his gaze as he turned and briefly looked at her then offered his response.

'Where we come from, Sophie,' Bastiano responded as the car moved off, 'I do.'

CHAPTER THIRTEEN

THEY BOTH CHOSE to leave it there.

It was dark and late and, though she did not say it, there was certain relief as the car came out from the tunnel the trees provided and the Old Convent loomed close.

The old building really was a comforting sight.

'Where are we going?' Sophie asked as the car veered away from the main convent and took a cobbled path that led towards the ocean.

'Did you think I would put you in the cells?'

A small laugh, which Sophie hadn't known she had left in her, escaped. 'I honestly wouldn't mind.'

'Well, instead you are being sent to seclusion.'

'Sounds good to me.'

The car pulled up at the front of a large sprawling building and she thought of days gone by when the nuns must have come here on retreat. Thankfully nobody jumped out to open the car doors. In fact, Bastiano fetched her bag and carried it to the main door, which he opened.

'This is where you live?' Sophie checked as she stepped in for, even before she had properly looked, it was clear that this was a home.

'It is.'

'I thought you said I was being sent to seclusion.'

'This used to be it,' Bastiano told her. 'It is my favourite space.'

She could see why; it was, for want of a better word, stunning.

The stone walls held all the charm of yesteryear and there were unspoiled views of the ocean from the huge lounge and likely most of the rooms too. The furnishings were modern, though they blended in with the surroundings, and there was a huge leather couch that Sophie ached to simply stretch out on, but she was far from ready to be living with him.

'I want to be alone.'

'I thought you might. In fact, I was thinking of putting you into one of the more secluded suites we keep for royals and such.'

'Then why didn't you?'

Bastiano answered with a question. 'How long until you are due?'

'A couple of months—the end of March.'

'That's only six weeks away.' Bastiano said. 'And time apart doesn't seem to serve us well.'

She was exhausted, he could see, and it was not fair to discuss it tonight.

'I'll show you to your room.'

Sophie eyes widened, just a fraction but enough for Bastiano to see.

'I'm not a complete bastard, Sophie.'

'I never said you were remotely one.'

She never had, Bastiano recalled, as she followed him down a long corridor.

'You really can relax here,' he explained. 'You have your own pool...'

'Did the nuns used to swim?'

'No,' Bastiano said. He was in no mood to smile at one of her jokes, yet he almost did. 'I had them put in.'

It was such a far cry from anything she was used to.

Oh, it might once have been a place for deep contemplation and it would serve as the same now, only with a bed that looked like a cloud and a bathroom so huge that she might need a map to locate the exit.

'Do you want to eat with me?' He offered her a choice.

'No.'

'Then I shall have Karmela bring you supper and come and unpack your things.'

'I think I can manage that,' Sophie said. 'There's not much.'

'We'll sort that out soon.'

'I don't want you dressing me.'

'Fine.' Bastiano shrugged. 'Is there anything you need?'

'No.' Sophie shook her head and then, when she guessed he might feel it was his job to entertain her, she gave a tight smile. 'I might just have a bath and go to sleep.' There was, though, one question that she had for him. 'How did you find out,' Sophie asked, 'about the baby?'

'I told you, I found out you had come here looking for work.' He omitted to mention the frantic feeling that had prompted him to call Alim.

'I wanted something that was live-in.'

'How did your parents take it?'

'As I expected them to. We haven't spoken for a long time but last week they asked me over for dinner...'

'That's good.'

'Not really. The priest was there to tell me about a lovely couple who would give my baby everything that I couldn't.'

He didn't need to guess what her response had been.

'I'm tired, Bastiano.' She really was. Yes, tonight she was supposed to have been working, but now she felt as if she had been unplugged from a fading battery and her energy had simply run out. 'Can this wait until morning?'

'Of course.'

To show Sophie how it all worked, he clicked on the intercom and was put straight through to Karmela.

'Could you send a light supper to the guest room?' he asked.

'Of course,' came the response. 'Anything else?'

'I'll just check.' He looked at Sophie, who shook her head. 'That will be all.'

'She'll be over soon,' he told Sophie.

'Thanks.'

'We can speak tomorrow night.'

'Tomorrow night?'

'I have to work. I lost a day today.'

'Sorry about that.'

Her sarcasm was wasted, for he had already gone.

It wasn't just Sophie who needed to be alone.

Bastiano too wanted to process the events of today. As soon as he had found out about the baby he had jumped in his car. The usual three-hour trip had taken two and he had been more focused on the practical—getting her out of the hell hole where she had lived and, yes, putting things right as speedily as could be arranged.

He poured a drink and lay on the bed, trying to wrap his head around the fact that he would soon be a father.

And that, had he not found out for himself, he might never have known.

He heard a car pull up outside and guessed that Sophie's supper was there.

Bastiano had no appetite.

A baby!

He had never considered fatherhood. When he had vaguely considered taking a wife his thought process had halted there.

In fact, he had heard a few weeks ago that Raul and Lydia were expecting and had silently thanked his lucky stars for the escape.

Bastiano lay there brooding for an hour at least, watching his bachelor life disappear before his eyes.

A knock on the door had him look up and there stood Sophie, her hair wet from a bath or shower and wrapped in a guest robe.

'Did you pack my pyjamas?'

'I packed everything that was there.'

'No, my pyjamas were under the pillow.'

'Well, I didn't go looking under your pillow! Who the hell wears pyjamas anyway?'

'I shared a bathroom with Pino,' Sophie said.

'Fair enough.' He nodded to his wardrobe. 'Take a shirt if you want one, though I've got my own bathroom and I shan't be peeping through the door.'

She smiled.

And not for the first time today.

But, then, that was what she did. Even in the middle of a row, there were some smiles.

And he returned it.

'I meant a clean one,' Bastiano said as she picked up his shirt from the floor.

'This will be fine. I hate starch.' And then she asked him something. 'It's your birthday?'

'How do you know?'

'Karmela said something when she brought my meal. You should have said.' Sophie gave a sweet smile. 'I'd have sent you flowers. But then again it might have given a mixed message.'

'Ha-ha,' Bastiano said, but as she walked off he had a parting shot. 'There will be no mixed messages from me.'

Good, Sophie thought, because sex was the last thing she needed to complicate things.

'Buon Compleanno.' Sophie shrugged and turned for the door, but it was Bastiano who had the last word.

'I still want you.'

No, he didn't deal in mixed messages.

To his own surprise, Bastiano's desire for her remained.

CHAPTER FOURTEEN

Sophie had no excuse for not sleeping well.

The supper had been delicious, her bath relaxing and the bed, when she had finally lain down on it, had felt like a cloud.

It was Bastiano who had unnerved her, though in the nicest of ways.

It had never entered her head that this far into pregnancy, and with so much to sort out, there would be such fierce attraction between them.

Sophie swung her feet to the floor and instead of cheap lino she felt the warmth of a thick rug. His home was so warm that there was no need to pull on a robe.

It was early, just before six, and she decided to go and get some milk and bring it back to bed.

She didn't expect to find him in the kitchen, dressed only in trousers and waiting for the percolator to fill.

'I thought you'd have your coffee brought to you in bed.'

'Not when I am here,' Bastiano said. 'I hate conversation in the morning.'

Sophie helped herself to some milk.

'How much prenatal care have you had?'

Always he surprised her. Sophie hadn't thought it the type of question he would ask so casually.

'I thought you didn't like conversation in the morning?'

'Some things have to be checked.'

'Not much,' she admitted.

'We have a doctor that visits daily. I'll get him to call in on you, though I think you should have the baby in Rome.'

'Rome?' Sophie gave an incredulous smile at his suggestion. 'Isn't there a hospital here?'

'Yes but you're not having the baby in Casta.' Bastiano shook his head.

'*I'll* decide where I'm having my baby.'

'*Our* baby,' he countered, but then he halted. He did not want to descend into a row but there was no way she was having the baby here. 'I'll have the doctor visit.'

'Well, let me know when,' Sophie said. 'I want to go into Casta. I need a few things for me as well as the baby. I was thinking of going to the market today.'

'In Casta?' He gave her an appalled look but Sophie just shrugged.

'You're turning into a snob, Bastiano.'

'I turned into one long ago,' Bastiano said. 'You are not dressing my baby from the Casta market. We'll speak tonight.'

He really didn't like conversation in the morning, Sophie thought, because without another word he took his cup and left her alone in the huge kitchen. Sophie headed back to bed and lay there watching the morning arrive over the ocean.

Yesterday's rain had gone, revealing a mild Sicilian winter's day.

Her favourite kind.

It didn't matter that she had hardly anything to wear because the morning was spent wrapped in a thick white robe.

The doctor came and he put her at ease straight away.

'It is busy over there!' He gave an eye-roll in the direction of the main building as he examined her. 'It is nice to have a straightforward pregnancy to take care of.'

'It doesn't feel very straightforward.'

'There is one baby, a healthy mother and a nice-sized baby. That's good news to me.'

She was thrilled to find out that the baby was a good size given her meals had been somewhat sparse.

'What do you deal with over there?' Sophie asked as he took blood to test. Since Karmela had mentioned a confidentiality clause, she had been dying to know what went on over at the Old Convent, but the doctor wasn't about to reveal anything.

'That would be telling tales. Believe me, young Sophie, you don't want to know.'

'But I do.'

After he had taken some blood, they discussed her having an ultrasound.

'Bastiano asked me to refer you to a colleague in Rome.'

'I haven't decided where I'm having the baby yet.'

'Well, without stating the obvious, I suggest you both work it out because babies keep to their own schedules. You could go into labour tonight and then the choice will be out of both your hands.' He gave her a lovely smile. 'Don't worry if you do, though, I've delivered a lot of babies.'

'It would be you who would deliver me?'

'It would be my privilege to.'

Sophie liked him.

He had salt-and-pepper hair and was patient with her endless questions; he didn't make her feel stupid or small.

And he was the first person who seemed genuinely pleased about the baby.

The rest of the morning was spent being pummelled by the resident masseuses, after which she sat on a lounger by the pool, so warm in her robe it was no surprise that she dozed off.

'Hey.'

She woke to his voice and looked up to a suited Bastiano.

'Is there no such thing as privacy?' Sophie asked.

'Privacy is not going to get us very far,' Bastiano said. 'I'm not going to be back until late tonight; work has piled up. What did the doctor say?'

'That everything is going very well.'

'What else?'

'He took some blood.'

'And?'

Sophie knew exactly what he was there for. Bastiano wanted to ensure that his instructions had been carried out.

Well, two could play at that game.

'He said that I am to go for an ultrasound in Casta tomorrow and that he would be thrilled to deliver me.'

She was surprised that he laughed.

So was he.

'You are such a liar.' Bastiano said.

He idly picked up the tie of her robe and as he did, the back of his hand brushed the baby bump beneath and then he turned so that his palm rested on the thick fabric.

'Sophie, please don't have the baby here. I couldn't stand it if anything went wrong.' He could feel the swell beneath his palm and then he looked up at Sophie and knew he simply could not bear it if something happened to either of them. 'If I can wrap things up here we can move into a hotel for a few weeks. Get married there…'

'In a hotel?'

'It's just a formality.' Even Bastiano knew he had said the wrong thing and he cursed himself as she removed his hand. The closeness that had almost appeared slipped back like the tide. 'Okay, we can get married in a church, I'm sure there are a few to choose from in Rome! I just don't want it to be born a bastard.'

'It's the twenty-first—'

'I'm aware of the century,' Bastiano interrupted. 'I want us married before the baby arrives.'

'I don't want to marry you,' Sophie said. 'I don't want a husband who doesn't love me.'

And she loathed that she fished, that she actually threw him a line, one that she hoped would see him pull her into his arms and tell her that of course that wasn't the case.

But Bastiano had long ago decided that his love was a dangerous gift and so he was rather caustic in his reply. 'It stopped being about you when you forgot to take your Pill.'

'Why couldn't I get pregnant by some bastard who just wrote me a cheque?'

'Do you really see us co-parenting, Sophie?' he asked. 'Do you think I am going to smile and nod at your new lover when I pick my child up for an access visit?'

'You could try.'

'If you wanted that then you should have found some new-age guy. I'm traditional. I'm Sicilian, for goodness' sake!'

'I want our child to grow up in a loving—'

'I can be loving.'

'I'm not talking about sex,' Sophie said.

Bastiano was.

He wanted to break the embargo and peel off her robe. Quite simply he was certain this was a dispute best settled in bed.

It was black-and-white to him.

'I want more from marriage,' Sophie said. 'I ran away because it wasn't love...'

'You ran away from a man who relied on your mother to cook for him,' Bastiano said, 'and now you have to settle for a virile billionaire. Boo-hoo.'

He stood and she lay there staring out at the ocean rather than look at him.

They were getting nowhere, Bastiano knew.

He had tried reason, he had tried religion, now he decided it was time to fall back on ways of old.

'How about we go out for dinner tonight?'

'I thought you had work.'

'I'll cancel it. We're going to go out tonight.'

'Are you asking me or telling me?' Sophie checked, and she saw the tightening of his jaw.

She was acting like a sulking princess, Sophie knew.

'We never did have our night out.'

'No,' Sophie said, 'I was too busy stealing your ring...'

'Sophie...' He halted but then he pushed himself to speak on. 'I know you didn't steal it.'

'Do you, now? And how's that?' She desperately wanted him to reply that it was because he knew she would never do that kind of thing. But he didn't.

'We'll speak tonight at dinner. I have a lot of work to get through but I should be through by five so be ready.'

'Five?' Sophie frowned. 'So early?'

'If I could have my PA reschedule the sun I would,' Bastiano said.

'Meaning?'

'I'll see you at five,' he told her. 'And please,' he added, 'do not buy anything from the market to wear! Your regular rags will do!'

He left her smiling.

In her worst mood, somehow he had made her smile.

And, he made her skin prickle.

Oh, the attraction had not faded for her, not a fraction, yet surely it must have for him.

It didn't feel as though it had.

A car drove her down the hill and it was indeed market day, for Casta was busy and it was nice to wander around.

There were signposts for the infirmary, where Bastiano was adamant that their baby would not be born. She passed a school and smiled at the sound of children's laughter.

There was the old courthouse, where Bastiano had told her Maria's will had been read.

It really was gorgeous, with an old hotel that had seen better days and a street lined with shops and cafés.

And it was exciting too because there were a couple of famous faces behind dark glasses in the café that Sophie went into, no doubt on day release from the Old Convent.

The owner greeted her warmly. 'Passing through?'

'No, I'm staying at the Old Convent.' Sophie smiled.

'Ah, a guest of Signor Conti.' The owner smiled. 'Then we need to find you a nice seat.'

He called to a waitress and she was guided to a table near the back. 'For you,' the owner said, and he brought her a large glass of hot blackcurrant without Sophie even looking at the menu. 'It is our house special and good for you,' he told her. 'And don't worry, no one will trouble you here, we'll keep an eye open.'

It took a moment or two to register that they thought she must be a *client*.

Bastiano really had done wonders, Sophie thought, for, unlike home, the town was a buzzing and happy place to be.

Sophie headed over to the church that had caught her eye when she had first passed through town.

It must be here that he had fought with Raul, Sophie guessed, and she slipped around the back to the grave-yard and read the inscriptions on the tombstones.

Gino Di Savo.

Raul's father, Sophie knew, and saw that he had died some ten years ago.

Next to him lay Maria, and Sophie wondered about the mind of a woman who would seduce a seventeen-year-old.

And then she turned and Sophie found what she was looking for. There she found out Bastiano's mother's name.

Philomena Conti.

Sophie felt her nostrils tighten when she saw the simple grave.

And then she saw the date of her death and Sophie did not even try to hold back the tears.

Philomena had died on the day that Bastiano was born.

Had Karmela not let on that it was his birthday yesterday, she might never have known. She understood the man a little more, and he was kinder than even she had given him credit for—even in their rows about their baby he had not scared her by telling her that his mother had died giving birth.

It was a sobering thought indeed.

And it was time, Sophie knew, to stop fighting.

She did have something to wear.

One thing.

Sophie stood in the little silver knickers she had pur-
chased on the day Rosa had persuaded her try on the
dress.

The over-dress she could not even get over her bust,
but the silver-grey underdress slid on.

It clung to every curve, yet somehow it revealed little,
for it fell to just on her knee and there was barely even a
glimpse of cleavage.

It was incredibly seductive, though.

For the first time in months Sophie added heels and
though she had very little make-up to work with, she
melted her mascara under a hot tap in order to reach the
last dregs and used a pen to dig out some lipstick.

Soon she saw his car approaching and Sophie was
suddenly nervous. She felt overdressed for Casta and the
small restaurants there.

Hell, she felt overdressed for five o'clock in Rome.

'Sophie!' Bastiano called out.

He wondered if she'd plead a headache to avoid dinner, but instead she stepped out confidently.

Bastiano had thought her like the sun on the day they'd
met.

Now a silver star emerged before the sky had even
darkened.

Her dress clung tightly to the baby they had made and
her legs seemed too fragile.

'Where are we going?' Sophie asked when he by-
passed the car.

'We're walking.'

Along the cobbled path on very high heels there was
little choice but to take his arm.

It was nice to walk.

'Am I overdressed?' she asked as they approached
the convent.

'Perhaps,' he said, 'but only because I prefer you in nothing.'

It was nice to flirt, but as they headed towards the restaurant nerves caught up.

'Will there be a lot of people?'

'I have twenty guests in residence,' Bastiano said as they walked in. 'And on my instruction, all are dining in their rooms tonight.'

Oh, it was heaven.

The tables were all candlelit and each candle had been lit for her. Even the stone walls were softened with thick white pillar candles but Bastiano steered her to the balcony. It had been dressed with care and a single table had been set up just for them.

'It is cool,' Bastiano said, 'even with heaters…'

'You're not eight months pregnant,' Sophie countered as she took a seat. 'I've forgotten what it is to be cool.'

'There's no wine list,' Bastiano said as he ordered bitter lemon for them both. 'My regular guests have no restraint.'

He made her laugh.

And then he made her want to cry.

'I owe you an apology,' Bastiano said, and he was suddenly serious. 'I was wrong to accuse you of taking my ring. I overreacted that morning. It was my mother's ring, it meant everything to me, and I had only just got it back from Raul.'

'From Raul?' Sophie frowned. 'Why did he have it?'

'I gave it to Maria.' He felt uncomfortable admitting it. 'She was wearing it when she died and all her jewellery was left to Raul. I don't think he even knew it was mine.'

'How did he find out?'

'When he asked for Lydia's address I said I would only give it to him if he returned the ring.'

Now she better understood his reaction that morning. It must have been hell to get it back, only to lose it.

'It was Inga who put the ring in your uniform.'

'Inga?' Sophie frowned. 'Did she confess?'

'Please,' Bastiano sneered, 'she has no conscience, she was still blaming you as they escorted her out.'

And he told her how Inga had shouted and sworn as she'd been walked out, remembering Sophie's quiet dignity in the same situation.

'I had Dario and Benita go over the CCTV footage. Inga must have…' He hesitated. He didn't want to embarrass her because he had realised that Inga would have heard them making love so he softened it a touch. 'She would have seen your uniform on the floor.'

It *was* cool outside; despite the heaters there was a chill from the ocean but the air suddenly seemed to blow warm on her skin as she recalled that morning and met his eyes.

'Do you think she heard us?'

'Who cares?'

'I do,' Sophie said, completely appalled. 'Though I shouldn't—she sleeps with guests.'

'That's shocking.' Bastiano pretended to shudder and then laughed. 'Thank God for the Ingas of the world.'

'You're terrible, Bastiano!'

'Oh, indeed I was.'

And instead of being cross, Sophie smiled and then she laughed because her name had been cleared, and it was the best feeling in the world.

Or amongst the best of feelings, because he was looking at her in that way again, a way that made her feel warm, a way that made the tiredness disappear and her body feel sensual and alive.

A waiter came out with a loaf of *mafalda*, which they tore and dipped in oil.

'The Contis and the Di Savos should have focused on making oil rather than feuding over wine,' Bastiano told her as they dipped their bread. 'They would have made their fortune.'

'The Contis and the Di Savos need to stop feuding, period,' Sophie said, referring to him and Raul.

'I agree.'

He was tired of it.

'Lydia is expecting too,' Bastiano told her.

'Your *almost* wife.'

She looked at him and knew that unrequited love was such a curse.

'The bread is fantastic,' Sophie said, to change the subject. She wondered if this would be her life, moving from topics to avoid hurt. Discussing the weather and the food on the table, rather than the hole he had shot through her heart.

'You can't get better than here,' Bastiano responded.

'Not true,' Sophie said. 'The chef at the Grande Lucia made the best...'

'Can I tell you something?' Bastiano said, and leant closer. She met his eyes and she knew she was in the path of a seducer, for his mouth had that smile and his eyes made her burn, and instead of fighting him Sophie let herself be played, for there were worse things she could think of than being seduced by Bastiano.

'Tell me,' she said, and tore another strip of bread.

'I stole the chef from the Grande Lucia. He is the one cooking for us tonight.'

'You stole Alim's chef?' She started to laugh.

A real laugh, because so skilled was she that at times she forgot his game.

'Of course. When I withdrew my offer I had my PA contact your chef with an offer he could not refuse. Now, instead of feeding the hordes in Rome, he has a maximum guest list of twenty-two to cater for. Staff too...'

'Your staff get meals?'

'Of course.'

'Five-star meals?' Sophie asked, as in front of her was placed a dish of *busciate*, Sicily's finest pasta dressed in a light almond sauce.

'Everyone deserves to be looked after,' Bastiano said. 'Not just the guests. That is why my retreats work so well.'

'It's amazing,' Sophie said. 'You should be very proud.'

'I am,' Bastiano said. 'People accuse me of bulldozing treasures but that is because I don't allow the interiors to be photographed—I don't need the publicity. The retreats I offer are for the guests to enjoy.'

And tonight that pleasure was exclusive to Sophie.

Tiny lights started to dance as dusk fell and she found out what he had meant about not being able to reschedule the sun, for it had turned to fire and was mirrored in the ocean.

'Dance?' Bastiano said as soft music came on.

It had been months since they had been in each other's arms, and so much had changed, yet they melded together like they had never been apart. Sophie wrapped her arms around his neck, swaying in his arms.

He looked right into her eyes and then she closed her eyes to his kiss.

She had forgotten the taste of perfection.

How with that mouth he made magic.

How the heat from his palm in the small of her back made her fingers press into the back of his head. And how the feel of him aroused her and could make her forget her cares.

She felt feverish, being held by him, dancing with him, being seduced by him.

His kiss was perfection.

It made her crave him and it made her feel weak.

'Why do you resist us?' Bastiano asked.

In his arms, she didn't know the answer to that.

'Come on,' he told her. 'I'm taking you home.'

CHAPTER FIFTEEN

THEY WALKED IN the dark but the moon was bright and the stars lit the night. They held hands as if they had been lovers for life.

'I love it here,' she said, because it was far safer than saying 'I love you'. She kept things light, determined not to reveal the ache in her heart. 'I went to one of the cafés in town and they thought I was one of your clients,' Sophie admitted, and she started to laugh. 'I'm trying to work out what they thought I was in rehab for.'

'They would have thought you were the partner of an errant actor,' Bastiano said. 'We sometimes have wives and girlfriends take a little holiday while their husbands straighten out.'

'Really?' she asked, as they reached the door and he gave her a light kiss, but one that made her toes curl.

'Really.'

'Who?'

'I can't tell you that,' Bastiano said.

They were stood at the door and she could hear the waves, and she knew that this was the moment.

'At least not until you marry me.'

Bastiano did it by the book.

Well, he didn't go down on bended knee but he took

out a black box and her throat was tight as he opened the clasp.

And there it was.

The proof that he did not love her.

Oh, the ring was stunning.

A diamond so huge that if she reached out and plucked a star from the sky it would surely sparkle just as brightly.

And in that moment she knew she would never matter to him the way she wanted to, because it wasn't the ring that meant everything to him.

'Isn't there something missing here, Bastiano?'

He knew exactly what she was referring to.

'Do you know why people think I'm such a bastard?' he said, and when she didn't answer he told her. 'Because I don't say things that other people want to hear.'

It was a terrible proposal because a big salty tear fell to her cheek. 'Sometimes it's kinder to lie,' she said.

'Not in this.'

If they were going to be honest, she would tell him how much this hurt. 'You gave Maria your mother's ring.'

'And look how that ended up!' He did not understand that she would choose his mother's cursed ring over the diamond he had selected with such care. 'I threw away the old ring,' Bastiano told her. 'It was bad news.'

And he was so cold, Sophie thought, that he could dispose of the thing most valuable to his heart.

Where the hell would that leave her and their child? But then he told her something, something honest and true.

'I will do everything to make our marriage work. I will read every book so that I can be the best father I can possibly be...' Yet still he saw tears. 'Sophie...' He told her the real truth. 'Believe me, you don't want my love.'

With a sob, she brushed past him and rushed straight to her room.

Believe me, she wanted to shout out, *I do*.

Instead, she stood with heart hammering and a body still alive from his touch and his kiss, loathing this one-sided love while knowing it was time to step up.

Of course they would marry.

Bastiano would be a wonderful father and even without his love it could be a wonderful marriage too, for she knew he cared for her.

He had proved it today, for even when arguing he looked out for her—not once had he hinted that his mother had died giving birth.

Bastiano was kinder and fairer than he knew and she knew she loved him.

And there was desire.

Such desire.

So she was stuck with the virile billionaire.

Boo-hoo!

Even with a heart breaking, just the thought of him made her smile. She wanted a slice of that dark, guarded heart, even if it could never be hers to own entirely. Sophie was starting to understand that there was a side to Bastiano she would never be allowed to know.

That privilege had been Maria's and she was through trying to compete with a ghost.

All she could be was herself.

And she would make her own rules.

She kicked off her shoes because they hurt, but it meant that her approach to his room was silent.

Bastiano lay on the bed with his hands behind his head, just as she had first found him, only he was dressed and sulking now.

'If we marry,' Sophie said, and Bastiano looked over to

where she stood at the door, 'it is to be here. If our child is going to be raised in Casta then I want to be married in the church. It is more than a formality to me.'

'Sophie…'

'Let me finish. If we are to marry then there is to be compromise. We can fly out straight after the service. I know it will take a couple of weeks to arrange…'

'I'll sort it,' Bastiano said.

He would.

'You just need a dress and to turn up.'

They would be married in the next forty-eight hours if it meant they could get the hell out of Casta and to the shiny equipment and slick obstetrician he had planned.

'I'll move out tomorrow,' he told her.

'Move out?' Sophie gave a laugh. 'It's a bit late for that.'

'In that case, come here.'

And there was a burn in his eyes that made her both excited and nervous at the same time. 'Should we wait for the wedding?'

'Do I look like Luigi?' he asked.

'No.' Sophie smiled and came over.

She sat down on the bed, as she had on the morning they had met. His hand found hers and then he felt the ripe swell of her stomach.

He could feel the kicks their baby gave and it was both mind-blowing and then calming because while inside her their baby was safe.

'I'm going to take such good care of you both.'

His voice was husky and thick with emotion and even if it wasn't love she knew his words came from the heart.

'I know that.'

Just as she had on that very first day, she leant over only this time she went straight for his mouth.

It was a deep and sensual kiss but an unhurried one, and he guided her so that she sat on his stomach.

'Back again,' he told her.

Only now there was a baby between them and a wedding to arrange. It was both the saddest and happiest night of her life.

Sophie could see the glint of her ring as she undid his tie and opened his shirt. She bent her head and they kissed long and slow, his hands sliding over the silver dress.

'I found out I was pregnant on the day I got this,' she said as he found the tiny, invisible zipper she had failed to spot when she had first tried it on.

He slid the zipper down and then pulled the dress up and over her head. Her breasts were full and encased in lace, and he stroked them through the fabric, then tipped her forward so he could taste with his mouth.

His fingers unclipped it and with it hanging on her arms his mouth met her flesh. It was the touch of a tongue that could make her weep and the nip of teeth that could have her beg.

So wanting was she that her sex was on his hands as he dealt with his belt and zipper and then there was the giddy bliss of him guiding her on.

'You and me,' he said, but did not finish.

Not because he did not want to say things at night that would fade with the dawn but because his love, Bastiano was sure, was a toxic curse.

But when they were together, life seemed to work.

And right now they were together.

Sophie could feel the gentle guidance of his hands as he held her hips and the dig of his fingers in her buttocks as he fought to hold back.

Her thighs gripped him and she ground down, causing a shiver to run through her body, but it felt like fire as she met his eyes.

He thrust up into her softly engorged grip and she leant her hands on his chest. Now there was nothing to hold back, for he knew of her love and so she cried his name when she came.

And he moved her then at whim and shot high into her.

It was deeply intimate and the most intense climax of his life, laced as it was with her name.

They lay there afterwards with his hand on her stomach and she felt it roam across her bump.

'It's asleep,' she told him, and soon so was she.

In the deep of night the baby awoke.

Sophie didn't notice.

Bastiano did.

He felt the wave of movement beneath his palm and then an unmistakable kick and he knew he was holding the future.

Not just the baby's but Sophie's too.

And he would do all he could to give his baby's mother the wedding she deserved.

CHAPTER SIXTEEN

'*Buongiorno, signor.*'

Bastiano did not answer the cheery greeting.

The best room in the best hotel in Casta was nowhere close to the twelfth floor at the Grande Lucia. The maid ignored the flick of his wrist to dismiss her and instead set about opening the drapes.

'It's a beautiful day to get married,' she told him.

Thank goodness it was today!

Bastiano had been away from the Old Convent for two nights and he itched to get back.

Not literally.

The Casta Hotel wasn't that bad!

He missed home.

Only that wasn't right, because as soon as the wedding was over they were flying to Rome and he was looking forward to that.

It was being so close to the street that irked, Bastiano decided.

Bastiano had never missed anyone in his life, so he had not worked out yet that he simply missed his future bride.

The pall that had hung over him for months was back and surely it was not how a groom should feel on his wedding day.

A trophy wife would be easier, Bastiano thought as

he showered in less than sumptuous surroundings. Yes, a nice trophy wife would have demanded a high-class wedding instead of the local church.

He pulled on black jeans and a jumper but found that he was grinning as he wondered how Sultan Alim and Gabi were faring down the hall.

Certainly this was no palace.

Though he had agreed to a low-key wedding, Bastiano had decided that Sophie deserved more than the basics.

Her family would be there but so to would Gabi and Alim.

And it would seem the entire valley would join them too.

Word was out and the joy at the upcoming nuptials was genuine.

As well as that, a couple of A-list guests at the Convent had applied for day leave.

It was turning into the wedding of the year and Sophie had no clue.

He took a walk down to the baker's rather than think about why he was doing all this for her.

The church was dressed for the occasion with flowers and ribbons and, out of sentiment more than habit, Bastiano walked around the side to the cemetery.

Even if it was just a formality, it was, after all, his wedding day.

But as he turned the corner a man looked over and Bastiano felt his hackles rise.

Raul Di Savo.

Here, after all that had passed between them.

But this time Raul did not leap across tombstones to attack him; instead, he stood stock-still as this time it was Bastiano who made his way over.

'I'm guessing that you're not here for the wedding.'

'No, I only just heard about that.' Raul gave a tight smile. 'Today is my mother's birthday.'

'Oh,' Bastiano said, and his first thought was that Sophie might freak if she found out he had arranged that they marry on Maria's birthday.

Bastiano hadn't known, though.

He looked at the tombstone, just as he had many times, and sure enough Maria's birthdate was etched there.

'I hear you are soon to be a father,' Bastiano said, and Raul nodded.

'Lydia is back in Venice. She's due in a few weeks.'

'Sophie too.'

Bastiano turned and walked away and stood for a moment at his own mother's grave.

There was no peace to be had here.

Had she even known she had a son?

Today it mattered, because a few weeks from now he would have a child of his own and there was a sudden need to put things right, to end feuds of old. He could hear the crunch of gravel as Raul walked off, and then the more rapid crunch of his own footsteps as this time it was Bastiano who strode towards him.

'Raul!' he called out, and watched Raul's shoulders stiffen before he turned around.

'Why did you refuse to hear my side?' He stared at the man who had once been a friend. 'Was it because I wasn't family?'

For a moment Bastiano thought history was about to repeat itself, that he would again meet Raul's fist, and he had a brief vision of trying to explain why he had chosen today, of all days, to confront his nemesis…

Except there would be no fighting today.

'Not here,' Raul said. Together, they walked up the hill

and sat on the ground outside the convent, where as boys and young men they had wasted many days.

They sat at first in silence, but it was Raul who finally spoke. 'I didn't *want* to hear your side. It was easier to blame you...'

'I guess,' Bastiano said. He had learned from the cradle that family came first.

'I always covered for her.'

Now the trees rustled, now the bird song seemed to fade as Bastiano learned there had been others.

Many others.

And beneath his feet the earth seemed to shift and then resettle as he chased the thoughts around his mind.

'I know now you didn't go there to seduce her,' Raul said. 'I just wasn't ready to hear it at the time.' And then he looked Bastiano right in the eyes. 'I apologise. When I found out she had taken your ring...'

Bastiano was about to correct him, to say that she hadn't taken it, he had given it to her, but that had been a trick of his mind. A trick Maria had played well.

'If you love me you would want me to have nice things.'

It hadn't been love.

Maria had told him that it was, and with nothing with which to compare it, he'd believed her.

'My mother had many lovers. I don't even know if Gino was my father,' Raul admitted. 'He married her just because she was pregnant...'

'He did the right thing at least.'

'No.' Raul shook his head. 'He resented the hell out of us. No one should marry because...' He halted, perhaps unsure of Bastiano's circumstances.

'I love Sophie.'

He knew he should have told her first, but he had only just realised it himself.

Love *did* make you smile.

Because on the morning of his wedding, as he reshuffled the truths of his past, just the thought of her was a comfort. It was Sophie he missed, Bastiano knew, not the walls of home.

'I'm sorry,' Raul apologised again. 'I wasn't insinuating that you didn't love. I was just saying how things sometimes—'

'No,' Bastiano broke in. 'You're right. I haven't told Sophie.' He looked over to the Old Convent and thought of her preparing for her wedding and not knowing how he felt. 'In fact,' he told Raul, 'I told her that I never could love her.'

'Then you need to call her now.'

'Merda!' Bastiano said as he tossed his phone, and they might have been teenagers again, for Bastiano had his foot in Raul's hands and was trying to get a leg up to scale a wall, but there was glass and wire at the top—his security was good enough to keep out even the hungriest press. He had to get to Sophie.

'You need to get changed,' Raul said, when Bastiano had no choice but to give in. 'You get married soon.'

To a bride who didn't know he loved her.

CHAPTER SEVENTEEN

BASTARD!

Sophie sat in the back of the bridal car with her father and watched as the priest signalled for them to go around.

He was late for his own wedding!!

Perhaps that was why he had been calling, Sophie thought, trying to fight the tears that were threatening.

To call things off.

She took a deep breath as the car slowly drove up the hill and she wasn't sure if it was the tightening in her stomach that made her gasp or the sight of a very dishevelled groom running towards the church with, Sophie was sure, his nemesis beside him.

The priest was now all smiles since the groom had arrived. But as she stepped out another pain hit.

Thankfully both her father and the priest thought it was nerves and that she was merely composing herself when she reached the church door and stood silent for a moment.

The church was full, that was all she saw.

And she was in labour.

If Bastiano could be late for his own wedding Sophie was quite sure he would be only too willing to call the whole thing off if he knew.

And she wanted to be married now, before the baby arrived.

Which meant she just had to grin and bear it!

The pains weren't too bad, and they were ages apart; first babies took a long time, the doctor had told her.

So she walked down the aisle, and blinked as a very famous actress gave her an encouraging smile, and a rap artist too.

What was going on?

And there was Gabi and Alim, and her heart was on fire as she walked towards the man she loved and always would.

She let in the sun, Bastiano thought as she walked towards him.

Here, in this church, where there had been so much darkness and pain, it was awash with colours and smiles.

It was way too late for white, so her dress was cream, with pale mint-green edging, just like the tiny roses she wore in her hair.

She had chosen her dress and flowers as if all this time he had loved her and wooed her.

And so badly he did love her.

And when he said his vows they were heartfelt and right, and Bastiano knew he could never have made it with a trophy wife, for it would have been over with by now.

'I will love you all the days of my life,' he told her, and he stared deep into her eyes, but Sophie's were slightly narrowed with suspicion.

'I really do love you,' he whispered, as he slid the ring on her finger.

Please, don't lie, Sophie thought, for his words sounded heartfelt and she couldn't bear the illusion, not on her wedding day. Her words were the same, though she paused midway as a pain hit and he gripped her fingers tight.

Bastiano knew.

He had seen her standing at the entrance and had read the pain behind her smile. His instinct had been to call off the wedding, but he knew how important it was to her.

'Perhaps,' he said in a low voice to the priest, 'we can do the shorter form…'

It was indeed a quick service and the bells rang out in Casta as the bride and groom emerged.

The past was gone, Bastiano knew.

Almost.

He looked over to the cemetery where his mother lay and he wanted them out of the valley now and into the waiting helicopter.

There would be no cake for the bride and groom.

'Look!' Gabi was holding up a ring. 'Look what I found in the gravel!'

Was it a sign?

His mother's blessing?

Sophie certainly seemed to think so for she slipped the ring on her finger, and though he smiled and shook hands with the guests, Bastiano felt as if he had been drenched in ice.

'We'll go to the chopper,' he told her, but Sophie shook her head.

'I don't think there's time.'

'Sophie…' Fear clutched at his heart and all he could see was that damn ring on her finger, not the wedding band or the engagement ring he had given her but the one that meant death.

'Why don't you go to the infirmary and let them check her?' Gabi suggested. She was used to drama at weddings and keeping things under control. 'If they say there is time to transfer then you can go from there.'

'Good luck,' Raul said, and shook his hand. 'You deserve it.'

A car drove them through the valley and the short distance to the infirmary but Sophie had plenty of questions on the way.

'You were late.'

'I was trying to get to you.'

'How come Raul was your best man?'

Oh, how she wanted to know, but there was so much pain she gripped his hand tight and knew the world was going to have to wait.

The scent of the hospital made him feel ill.

They walked through the maternity unit and past the nursery where babies cried and to a very small delivery suite where it seemed a cast of thousands was gathered.

Well, actually, there were four, Bastiano counted, but he was not about to say what he had to with this audience present.

'Could I speak to my wife alone, please?'

'I'm having our baby here,' Sophie shouted, because she was so pleased to see her salt and pepper doctor and his kind smile. 'I don't want to go to Rome!'

'*Signor...*' A midwife who introduced herself as Stella asked if she could have a word outside.

She was elderly and kind as she told him there was no question that Sophie be transferred.

'She is soon to have the baby,' Stella said. 'Your wife is ready to push. You need to stay calm for Sophie.'

'I am calm,' he told her.

Bastiano was.

No one knew him.

No one really could.

For he had never allowed anyone to get close. It was a strange and unfamiliar sensation to want to draw Sophie close now.

Bastiano had accepted back in the car that their baby would soon be here and he was not about to add to the drama.

The midwife seemed to think otherwise.

'Bastiano,' Stella said, 'I was here when you were born and so I understand why you are worried for Sophie, but there isn't time to transfer her now...'

'There is time for me to speak with my wife alone, though?'

'For a moment, yes.'

'A moment is all I need.'

Sophie watched as he walked in and the doctors and nurses were called out and then Bastiano closed the door.

'I love you,' he told her.

'Bastiano...' she begged. 'Please, don't do this. You loved Maria.'

'No, she told me that I did and I had nothing to compare it to, and so I believed her. You were right, I was seventeen, and I had no idea what love was.

'I love *you*,' he said. 'Like I never have before or ever could another.'

He would never say such a thing to please someone else, Sophie knew that.

And so she knew it was the truth that she heard.

It was love, and she could feel its fierce embrace, a grip stronger than the pain that engulfed her.

Stella's encouragement was needed, for despite Sophie's slender frame it would seem that she grew big babies.

Bastiano's support was needed too, so he looked not at an emerald and seed pearl ring on her finger but deep into her eyes and told Sophie, when she was sure that she couldn't, that, yes, she could, and that with one more push their baby would be here.

'Make that two,' Bastiano said.

Yes, she grew big babies.

With broad shoulders and a long frame.

And Bastiano watched as his son unfurled and was delivered onto Sophie's stomach, his lusty cries filling the room.

'His father was the same.' Stella laughed as their baby refused to settle. 'I used to stay at the end of my shift to give him a cuddle.' She smiled as she helped Sophie to feed her baby and then there was calm.

He was such a beautiful baby, with long lashes and straight black hair, and finally the shock of his early entrance to the world turned to peaceful slumber in his mother's arms.

The hell of the last few months was gone.

'*Complimenti*, Signora Conti,' a domestic said as she brought in a very welcome meal.

'I can't get used to my name.' Sophie laughed as Bastiano held the baby and she ate brioche and drank warm milk laced with nutmeg.

'There are two names you have to get used to,' Bastiano said, gazing at his son. 'Have you decided on his yet?'

'No.'

She had never known such happiness and later in their little room on the maternity ward they watched the sun set over Casta on their wedding day and the birth day of their son.

'Here.'

Bastiano cracked open a bottle and Sophie had her first, long-awaited taste of champagne, smiling when Stella came in to check on them.

'You have had a lot of phone calls,' Stella informed then. 'There is a big party going on in town.'

'What time do you finish?' Bastiano asked.

'Midnight.'

Sophie handed Bastiano their baby, who was now content, and she watched as he placed him in the little Perspex cot.

'I'm tired,' Sophie said.

'Sleep.'

'You'll stay?'

'Of course.'

It was an exhausted sleep that she fell into and it was after midnight when she woke and there was a frantic moment because neither her baby nor Bastiano was there.

Sophie put on a gown and headed out, past the delivery suite, and she came to the nursery and saw Bastiano sitting there, their baby in his arms, talking with Stella.

She heard a cry from her baby and watched as Stella held out her arms and Bastiano handed him over.

They were talking, deep in conversation, and Stella looked in no rush to go anywhere, despite the fact her shift was over.

Something told Sophie not to approach. For Bastiano to be sitting talking so intently made her certain that Stella was saying something he might just need to hear.

She went back to her room and lay watching the moon drift across the sky and the surf crash onto the rocks. She hoped that there could be some resolution for her husband, for he had made his peace with the past, but there was so much still missing.

'Hey.'

It was a long time before he came back and his face was like marble in the moonlight, his scar vivid, and she could hear the strain in his voice, though he carried on as if everything was normal. 'He is hungry again.'

She fed their not so tiny baby and tried to work out a name for him.

'I can't decide,' Sophie said, when they had nailed it down to the final two. He slept in her arms and made little contented noises, barely murmuring when Bastiano took him and placed him in the cot.

Then he came back to the bed and took her in his arms, breathing in the scent of her hair, and a world that had gone off kilter tipped back to delicious normality again.

'Stella was with my mother when she had me.' He told her of the conversation he had had. 'I always thought she died giving birth but it wasn't until after...'

'So she knew she had had a son?'

She felt him nod and they held each other. 'She chose my name. It means respected man, and that was what she wanted for me, even though she was not married.'

'She chose appropriately,' Sophie said, for Bastiano was very respected in Casta now.

'Apparently, she had a heart attack, her blood pressure kept going up. During the birth she kept calling out for my father...' He was the closest in his life he had ever been to tears, but he fought them, and then he told her the truth he had just learnt. 'He couldn't come, of course, as he had a wife and son. I've just found out that Raul is my brother.'

She peeled herself from his arms and during a conversation where there were no smiles to be had, Sophie found one.

'Half-brother,' she said. 'There is a very important half, for Maria was not your mother.'

'No.' He smiled. 'Certainly not.'

CAROL MARINELLI   183

And he told her what he had gleaned, for his mother had cried through the long delivery with the young student midwife.

'She and Gino were dating a little but she wanted to save herself for marriage. Maria decided she wanted Gino and gave him what my mother refused to. Maria got pregnant so he married her, but it would seem he had loved my mother all along. She gave in and slept with him and an affair commenced, but by then he had a wife and a son. He loved her, I think, he gave her this ring...'

'What about you?' Sophie asked. 'Did he love you?'

He let out a long breath. 'He blamed me for her death, and apparently he took one look at me and walked out.'

'Do you think Maria knew?'

'I think she seduced me the same way she seduced my father,' Bastiano said. 'I think I reminded her of him and to get back at her husband for not loving her, she left her money to his son...'

'And look what you did with it,' Sophie said.

For he had fought his way back to respect, and turned ruins into beauty.

They shared a kiss, and there was peace when he lay on the bed beside her. They stayed up to watch the night disappear and light fill the sky.

'Call Raul,' she told him.

'It's too early.'

'I would think this news is thirty-two years late.'

So she lay there and listened to Bastiano as he told Raul the news. That they were more than friends, and even as enemies they had been tied to each other and unable to walk away, for they were brothers.

Which meant there were more questions as they worked their way back into each other's lives.

'Yes,' Bastiano said, 'we have a name.' And he looked over at Sophie as he said his son's name out loud. 'Rafael.'

They had chosen appropriately for it meant God has healed.

He had.

EPILOGUE

THERE WAS NO place nicer for afternoon tea than at the Grande Lucia and Sophie did not have to be asked twice before she said yes.

Lydia and Raul were coming in from Venice and Gabi and Alim were in residence, so what better excuse than to fly to Rome and catch up with friends?

Ronaldo greeted them warmly and Anya waved. What bliss to sink into a leather chair and eat the pretty cakes and to laugh and catch up.

Raul and Lydia had a daughter, Serena, just a few days younger than her cousin Rafael, and little Lucia was a delight, the boss of the babies, they all agreed.

Oh, Sophie loved being back here.

There was a soothing familiarity to the place and she was thrilled that Gabi had persuaded Alim not to sell it.

It was almost a second home.

She looked over at Bastiano, who was holding their son, and to see him laugh at something Raul said made her heart swell.

Yes, Sophie was a thief for she had stolen his heart and she treated it with such tender care, as he did the same for hers in return.

Familia.

Absolutely.

They had been born to love each other, she was certain of that.

'Are you staying?' Gabi asked.

'Of course.' Sophie smiled. 'I just wish they hadn't fired Inga and she could serve me breakfast in bed.'

Oh, that would be perfect, but she could more than live without it.

It was a wonderful catch-up and afternoon tea stretched into dinner, so it was late in the night when Bastiano took Rafael through to the nursery and placed him in his crib while Sophie got ready for bed.

'Sophie,' Bastiano called to her, for she was taking ages and now that the baby was asleep it was time to crack open champagne.

'One moment.'

He poured two glasses and placed hers by the bed. The turndown service had been in and he was just about to get up from bed and open the drapes and shutters for the view when Sophie emerged from the bathroom.

She was wearing her old uniform and her hair was up in a messy bun. She always made him smile.

First she opened the drapes and the shutters and stood a moment to take in the view, and to take in her life, for it was everything she had hoped for and more.

'Get over here,' he told her.

'I'm just preparing the view for you, Signor Conti,' she told him, and turned around and smiled. 'Then I am going to make the bed...with you in it.'

Yes, the words were out, and she had let them out, and they were how she felt.

They loved each other so.

* * * * *

*If you enjoyed this final instalment of
Carol Marinelli's*
BILLIONAIRES & ONE-NIGHT HEIRS *trilogy
don't forget to read the first two parts*

*THE INNOCENT'S SECRET BABY
BOUND BY THE SULTAN'S BABY
Available now!*

MILLS & BOON®
Hardback – July 2017

ROMANCE

The Pregnant Kavakos Bride	Sharon Kendrick
The Billionaire's Secret Princess	Caitlin Crews
Sicilian's Baby of Shame	Carol Marinelli
The Secret Kept from the Greek	Susan Stephens
A Ring to Secure His Crown	Kim Lawrence
Wedding Night with Her Enemy	Melanie Milburne
Salazar's One-Night Heir	Jennifer Hayward
Claiming His Convenient Fiancée	Natalie Anderson
The Mysterious Italian Houseguest	Scarlet Wilson
Bound to Her Greek Billionaire	Rebecca Winters
Their Baby Surprise	Katrina Cudmore
The Marriage of Inconvenience	Nina Singh
The Surrogate's Unexpected Miracle	Alison Roberts
Convenient Marriage, Surprise Twins	Amy Ruttan
The Doctor's Secret Son	Janice Lynn
Reforming the Playboy	Karin Baine
Their Double Baby Gift	Louisa Heaton
Saving Baby Amy	Annie Claydon
The Baby Favour	Andrea Laurence
Lone Star Baby Scandal	Lauren Canan

MILLS & BOON®
Large Print – July 2017

ROMANCE

Secrets of a Billionaire's Mistress	Sharon Kendrick
Claimed for the De Carrillo Twins	Abby Green
The Innocent's Secret Baby	Carol Marinelli
The Temporary Mrs Marchetti	Melanie Milburne
A Debt Paid in the Marriage Bed	Jennifer Hayward
The Sicilian's Defiant Virgin	Susan Stephens
Pursued by the Desert Prince	Dani Collins
Return of Her Italian Duke	Rebecca Winters
The Millionaire's Royal Rescue	Jennifer Faye
Proposal for the Wedding Planner	Sophie Pembroke
A Bride for the Brooding Boss	Bella Bucannon

HISTORICAL

Surrender to the Marquess	Louise Allen
Heiress on the Run	Laura Martin
Convenient Proposal to the Lady	Julia Justiss
Waltzing with the Earl	Catherine Tinley
At the Warrior's Mercy	Denise Lynn

MEDICAL

Falling for Her Wounded Hero	Marion Lennox
The Surgeon's Baby Surprise	Charlotte Hawkes
Santiago's Convenient Fiancée	Annie O'Neil
Alejandro's Sexy Secret	Amy Ruttan
The Doctor's Diamond Proposal	Annie Claydon
Weekend with the Best Man	Leah Martyn

MILLS & BOON®
Hardback – August 2017

ROMANCE

An Heir Made in the Marriage Bed	Anne Mather
The Prince's Stolen Virgin	Maisey Yates
Protecting His Defiant Innocent	Michelle Smart
Pregnant at Acosta's Demand	Maya Blake
The Secret He Must Claim	Chantelle Shaw
Carrying the Spaniard's Child	Jennie Lucas
A Ring for the Greek's Baby	Melanie Milburne
Bought for the Billionaire's Revenge	Clare Connelly
The Runaway Bride and the Billionaire	Kate Hardy
The Boss's Fake Fiancée	Susan Meier
The Millionaire's Redemption	Therese Beharrie
Captivated by the Enigmatic Tycoon	Bella Bucannon
Tempted by the Bridesmaid	Annie O'Neil
Claiming His Pregnant Princess	Annie O'Neil
A Miracle for the Baby Doctor	Meredith Webber
Stolen Kisses with Her Boss	Susan Carlisle
Encounter with a Commanding Officer	Charlotte Hawkes
Rebel Doc on Her Doorstep	Lucy Ryder
The CEO's Nanny Affair	Joss Wood
Tempted by the Wrong Twin	Rachel Bailey

0717 GEN STD HB

MILLS & BOON®
Large Print – August 2017

ROMANCE

The Italian's One-Night Baby	Lynne Graham
The Desert King's Captive Bride	Annie West
Once a Moretti Wife	Michelle Smart
The Boss's Nine-Month Negotiation	Maya Blake
The Secret Heir of Alazar	Kate Hewitt
Crowned for the Drakon Legacy	Tara Pammi
His Mistress with Two Secrets	Dani Collins
Stranded with the Secret Billionaire	Marion Lennox
Reunited by a Baby Bombshell	Barbara Hannay
The Spanish Tycoon's Takeover	Michelle Douglas
Miss Prim and the Maverick Millionaire	Nina Singh

HISTORICAL

Claiming His Desert Princess	Marguerite Kaye
Bound by Their Secret Passion	Diane Gaston
The Wallflower Duchess	Liz Tyner
Captive of the Viking	Juliet Landon
The Spaniard's Innocent Maiden	Greta Gilbert

MEDICAL

Their Meant-to-Be Baby	Caroline Anderson
A Mummy for His Baby	Molly Evans
Rafael's One Night Bombshell	Tina Beckett
Dante's Shock Proposal	Amalie Berlin
A Forever Family for the Army Doc	Meredith Webber
The Nurse and the Single Dad	Dianne Drake

GEN STD LP

MILLS & BOON®

Why shop at millsandboon.co.uk?

Each year, thousands of romance readers find their perfect read at millsandboon.co.uk. That's because we're passionate about bringing you the very best romantic fiction. Here are some of the advantages of shopping at www.millsandboon.co.uk:

* **Get new books first**—you'll be able to buy your favourite books one month before they hit the shops

* **Get exclusive discounts**—you'll also be able to buy our specially created monthly collections, with up to 50% off the RRP

* **Find your favourite authors**—latest news, interviews and new releases for all your favourite authors and series on our website, plus ideas for what to try next

* **Join in**—once you've bought your favourite books, don't forget to register with us to rate, review and join in the discussions

Visit **www.millsandboon.co.uk**
for all this and more today!